The Witch of the Breton Woods

by

Jennifer Ivy Walker

The Witch of the Breton Woods

COPYRIGHT © 2024 by Jennifer Ivy Walker

Contact Information: info@thewildrosepress.com

Cover Art by *The Wild Rose Press, Inc.*

The Wild Rose Press, Inc.
PO Box 708
Adams Basin, NY 14410-0708
Visit us at www.thewildrosepress.com

Publishing History
First Edition, 2024
Trade Paperback ISBN 978-1-5092-5571-9
Digital ISBN 978-1-5092-5572-6

Published in the United States of America

Dedication

In memory of my late brother Jeff

A lifelong Boston Red Sox fan and history buff fascinated by World War II, Jeff would have been so proud to see his sister write a novel about the triumph of love, courage, and freedom under the oppression of the Third Reich

Chapter 1

The Wounded Soldier

Lavender and pink streaked the dawn sky, the fresh saline scent of the briny marsh cleansing the crisp morning air. Yvette stood in rubber boots, harvesting shellfish in a secluded cove, far from suspicious, watchful eyes. With a hammer and knife, she chiseled clusters of oysters and mussels attached to rocks along the shoreline, placing them in nearby buckets of brackish water. A net attached to a long handle enabled her to collect scallops from the seafloor amid the eelgrass in the estuary. And, taking advantage of low tide, she dug clams from the exposed mudflats above the recessed water of the Cancale Bay.

She continuously scanned the shoreline, her heart racing at the risk of being caught.

When she'd collected several dozen of the mollusks, she lugged her precious cargo back to shore where she transferred the shellfish to satchels lined with straw and packed with ice, strapped on either side of her borrowed mule. Climbing into the saddle, she headed away from the Breton shore toward the dense woods in which she lived and where she surreptitiously traded her valuable harvest with two intrepid neighbors. For if the Nazis or, worse yet, *les collabos*—the local French villagers who collaborated with the enemy and betrayed their own people—were to catch her, she would be imprisoned.

Tortured.

And executed.

Ever since the Nazis invaded France four years ago, food had become pitifully scarce, despite rations designed to ensure its supply and distribution. The German army diverted goods and crops to feed its Wehrmacht soldiers, and French citizens waited in long lines to spend coupons on whatever food was still available. More often than not, there was little to nothing left.

Yvette compensated for the lack of food by bartering her shellfish for precious commodities. Her neighbor, the baker Marcel Dubois, provided Yvette with grain for her hens, as well as flour, corn, oats, bread, and the use of his mule for transporting her harvest. In return, she paid Monsieur Dubois with oysters, mussels, clams, or scallops.

Another villager, Jacques Blanchard—an old farmer who tended sheep—supplied Yvette with lanolin, cheese, milk, and raw wool. She cleaned, combed, and spun the fleece to make blankets, sweaters, socks, and gloves, trading them wherever possible for necessities such as cooking oil, chicory, and potatoes. She was always on guard, for spies were everywhere.

And they all reported to Étienne Boucher. The most powerful of *les collabos* in the small seaside village of *le Vivier-Sur-Mer.*

A burly blond brute with a penchant for cruelty, Boucher—called the Butcher, the literal translation of his name but also an apt nickname for the atrocities he committed for the Gestapo—was a Section Leader in *La Milice,* the armed paramilitary organization charged with hunting and capturing Jews, members of the French Resistance, and anyone who opposed the strict, rigid policies imposed by the Third Reich. The Butcher and his *miliciens* enjoyed the steady pay, hefty rations, and unlimited power accorded them by the Nazi regime which placed them above the law and granted them impunity and immunity. Many of the French *collaborateurs* who colluded with the Nazis took advantage of their extra rations and profited from selling goods at exorbitant prices on the Black Market.

With kickbacks to Étienne Boucher and *la Milice* to look the other way.

Yvette, like many villagers in *le Vivier-Sur-Mer*, secretly bartered to avoid starvation.

And lived in constant, relentless fear of discovery.

"*Bonjour, Madame Dubois.*" Yvette rode the gentle mule toward a small stone cottage where her neighbor, the baker's wife, stepped out the front door to greet her. "I have some delicious oysters and clams for you today." Yvette dismounted, removed a satchel from the mule's pack, and handed it to the plump, middle-aged woman with graying hair and a suspicious scowl.

Marie-Claire Dubois wiped her hands on a grease-stained white apron, accepted the satchel, and poured the contents into a straw-filled basket. Her narrow eyes widened with delight at the sight of the fresh seafood. "*Merci beaucoup.* These look delicious."

Yvette removed the second satchel and slung it over her shoulder. The shellfish inside would provide her own dinner for the next three days. With a grateful smile, she handed the mule's reins to Madame Dubois. "Thank you for lending me Suzette. May I borrow her again on Friday? The tide will be low in the early morning—the perfect time to harvest shellfish. Would that be possible?"

Hesitant and mistrustful, Madame Dubois glanced nervously into the surrounding woods. "*I don't know…*" Reluctance edged her raspy voice. "Marcel and I *would* enjoy the extra seafood…" Her brows furrowed in concentration. "I suppose it would be all right. Wait here. I'll be right back." Madame Dubois led the mule into the backyard to graze, then scurried up the stone steps into her vine-covered cottage, lugging the basket of shellfish. She returned a few minutes later with two small sacks and a large, disc-shaped loaf of hearty, country bread.

"Here is the corn, a pound of flour, and a nice *pain de campagne.*" Madame Dubois handed a burlap bag, a cotton sack, and the multi-grain loaf to Yvette. "See you Friday morning. *Au revoir.*"

Her arms full, her body weighed down like a pack mule herself, Yvette said goodbye and trudged home, following the narrow dirt path into the thick forest.

As much as I hate to, I absolutely must make the trip into town on Friday. I need ice for the refrigerator and coal for the stove, and I have to use my rations for a few other supplies as well. If I time it just right, I can arrive mid-morning and hopefully avoid the Butcher. I hate the way he looks at me.

Like a hunter.

Or a hungry wolf.

A shiver of dread rippled up Yvette's spine. Étienne Boucher had lusted after her ever since she'd first come to *le Vivier-Sur-Mer* four years ago, when the Nazis confiscated her family farm.

And gunned down her father and three brothers before her very eyes.

She shuddered violently at the horrific, haunting memory.

German soldiers marching them to the edge of the woods…the jolting, explosive bursts of gunfire…their beloved, bloodied bodies collapsing among the wildflowers in the grass…

Low, agonized moaning interrupted Yvette's nightmarish reverie.

That's a man's voice. And it's coming from over there.

She followed the deep groans through a copse of trees to find an American soldier impossibly tangled in a nylon parachute. Suspended from a high branch of a massive oak tree, he was dangling upside down, hanging by an obviously broken leg. A sharp bone protruded from the torn, blood-soaked pants of his khaki uniform, and dried blood—which must have leaked from under his helmet—covered half of his contorted face. His pitiful wails pierced her heart.

I can't lower him to the ground by myself. He's twice my weight. And if I cut the ropes, he'll plummet headfirst. He already has a head injury, judging from the gore all over his forehead. Please, God, let him hang on until I get back.

"I'll go get help. I promise to come back soon." She called up to him, hopeful that he could hear her.

And that he understood French.

I have to fetch Jules and les Loups. They can help me get the soldier down from the tree and carry him into my cottage. I have my healing herbs… I can cleanse his head injury, set his broken leg, stitch up his wounds. But I'll have to keep him hidden from the Butcher and la Milice. Please let me get back to him before they do!

5

She hid her satchel of seafood and bags of supplies behind a log and covered them with branches and leaves. *I can run faster without this extra weight. But I'll hide it, so no one steals the food.*

With a quick glance to be sure she had not been followed, Yvette dashed off into the dense Breton woods.

****

The limestone cave was four miles away, burrowed into a heavily forested ledge, hidden by oak and beech trees whose thick foliage concealed it from view. The mouth of the cavern was camouflaged with leafy branches by the Resistance Group who used it as a refuge as well as a lookout point. The earthy scent of decaying leaves and rich black loam greeted Yvette as she gave the distinctive whistle to signal her arrival.

Her older brother Jules emerged from the trees, his scarred, handsome visage smeared with mud, his worn clothing as dark as the hair he'd hacked short with his jagged hunting knife. Now twenty-six, Jules had miraculously survived the merciless shooting by the Nazis that Yvette had witnessed four years earlier. Shot in the shoulder, he'd managed to crawl into the woods near their family farm, where he'd been rescued by the Resistance Group who called themselves *les Loups*—the Wolves. Named after the legendary lupines prevalent in the age-old tales of the enchanted Breton forest where they now lived as outlaws.

Hunted by the Gestapo.

La Milice.

And Étienne Boucher. The Butcher.

Yvette wove through the thick trees and dashed across the leafy terrain toward her brother who warily scanned his surroundings. "Jules," she gasped, breathless. "I've found a wounded soldier. I need your help getting him to the cottage where I can treat him. His parachute is all tangled up in a tree. He's hanging upside down, suspended by a mangled, broken leg. We need to save him before the Butcher finds him. Please...come with me now."

Jules gave a shrill whistle, like the keening cry of a hawk, and three other *Loups* clad in dark brown and black appeared in the woods near the bedrock cave. "Wounded soldier. Probably a survivor from the plane shot down last night." He turned to Yvette. "*Le Jour J.* D-Day. Thousands of Americans were dropped into Normandy yesterday. The German flak guns—88 mm antiaircraft cannons—shot down a bunch of Allied planes. Including one last night. That soldier must be American." With a swoop of his arm, he motioned for his fellow *Loups* to follow. "Let's get him before the Butcher does."

Briac, Gwilherm, and Pierrick—three members of *les Loups* who were her brother's closest friends—joined Jules in following Yvette through the forest back to the tree where the wounded American was hanging from his broken, horribly twisted left leg. Parachute cords were tangled in the upper branches of the huge oak, wrapped around his brown leather boot and lower leg. The pathetic soldier was suspended upside down, entangled in tattered remnants of white nylon. Although Yvette had heard him moaning earlier, the fact that he was silent now indicated that he was most likely unconscious.

"We can lower him over that branch like a pulley." Briac squinted, shielding his vision from the morning sunlight streaming through the leaves of the oak, as he pointed to a thick limb just below the wounded soldier. Beneath the thin mustache under his prominent nose, one side of Briac's mouth curled up in a sly grin. "I'm part monkey," he joked gruffly, "so I'll climb up and cut the cords. You catch him as I ease him down to the ground."

Bulky, bearded, and swarthy like a shaggy brown bear, Gwilherm positioned himself under the suspended soldier as Briac hoisted himself up into the tree, wrapping a section of the torn parachute around his waist and securing his torso to the trunk.

The sandy-haired Pierrick, built like a rock as his name implied, joined Gwilherm and Jules under the enormous oak branch which would be used as a pulley.

Heart pounding, legs trembling under her cotton dress, Yvette frantically searched the forest, expecting Étienne Boucher and *la Milice* to burst into view. Thankfully, there was no sign of them. Yet. She forced a swallow of temporary relief down her dry, constricted throat.

"OK…here he comes." Briac wrapped the bulk of the nylon parachute over the hefty oak limb, removed the hunting knife strapped at his waist, and cut the cords tangled around the soldier's ankle. Dodging the American's leg as it fell free, Briac leaned to the side and gripped the parachute, bolstering himself with legs wrapped securely around the branch where he sat, his back pressed against the enormous trunk of the tree.

As Briac slowly lowered the soldier to the ground, Gwilherm caught him under the shoulders, supporting the American's head against his broad chest. Pierrick grabbed hold of the soldier's good leg, and Jules caught the broken one by gripping the uninjured thigh.

Yvette spread the parachute material on the ground.

"Lay him on this. We'll use it to carry him to the cottage. Try not to jar his head."

Briac climbed down from the tree, wrapping the cut cords into a torn section of the parachute. He scanned the upper tree branches, scrutinizing their surroundings. He picked up a few scattered portions of debris, then—nodding in satisfaction—turned to the colleagues who were laying the soldier onto the parachute. "No trace left behind. Nothing for the Butcher to find. Let's move."

While Yvette retrieved her hidden satchel of seafood and bags of bartered supplies, *les Loups* positioned themselves around the wounded American soldier. Each of the four men carried a corner of the makeshift stretcher, following Yvette through the Breton woods to the small stone cottage covered with thick vines of ivy, hidden behind a profusion of low-lying oak branches and dense, overgrown shrubs.

"Bring him into the bedroom." Yvette opened the heavy wooden entrance door, indicating the narrow hall leading from the foyer to the room which had once belonged to Yanna's son. "Set him down on the floor so I can assess his injuries. I'll need your help getting him into the tub to wash off the mud." She hurried into the kitchen, dropped the food items onto the counter, and returned to close and bolt the front door. Fetching the tin tub from the storage pantry in the kitchen, she rolled it into the bedroom as they carefully laid the soldier onto the pinewood floor.

Yvette grabbed a towel from the armoire and used it to cover a pillow that she snatched from the bed. She knelt on the floor beside the injured soldier and carefully removed the helmet, cupping his head with her other hand to hold it as still as possible.

Clumps of dried blood and matted brown hair stuck to a large, swollen lump with torn skin on the right rear side of his skull. Yvette gently placed his head upon the pillow and unlaced the leather boot of his injured foot.

The severely swollen ankle was hideously discolored black and blue. A sharp bone protruded from the soldier's shin, the skin bloodied and blackened with dirt. Yvette cautiously lowered the injured foot to the floor and looked up at Jules, his lupine eyes dark and fierce. "I'll need two splints to set his leg. And crutches for him to move around once he regains consciousness." She rose to her feet and smoothed the lower half of her floral dress. "I'll fetch my tape measure. Take off his clothes—carefully—so I can see if he has any other injuries. I'll go pump water from the well and be back soon."

As she headed toward the bedroom door, Jules and Briac rolled the American onto his side to remove the supply pack strapped to his back. "Check to see if he has any identification." Jules handed the knapsack to Pierrick as Yvette left the room.

She returned a few minutes later with the cloth ruler and two buckets of water, which she poured into the metal tub. She'd need several more to sufficiently fill it for the soldier's bath.

Jules measured the American's lower leg for the splint and the distance from his armpit to the heel of his boot. "He's very tall. Close to two meters. We'll need long branches to make the crutches."

Yvette fetched two more buckets of water from the well in the backyard and poured them into the tub. She crouched down beside the unconscious, naked soldier, carefully examining him for broken bones or internal injuries. Her eyes roved over the muscular chest covered with brown hair, the trail leading down the rippled abdomen to the dark patch between his thighs. Aware of her brother's watchful presence, Yvette averted her gaze from the soldier's well-endowed body. "I'll fetch two more buckets of water. I need to wash his hair, the head wound, and the torn leg. I want to prevent them from getting infected."

When the tub was ready, she had the four *Loups* lift the wounded soldier and ease him into the water. "Keep his head stable." Yvette placed her hands behind the soldier's skull to steady it as Jules and the men lowered him in.

"Jules—stay here with Yvette. You can help her move him around. We'll go pump more water from the well and cut branches for the crutches and splints. Be back soon. Whistle if you need us." Briac led Pierrick and Gwilherm from the bedroom, through the kitchen, and out the back door.

Yvette poured water carefully over the American's head and lathered his hair. She spotted Briac in the backyard pumping water from the well.

I pray none of the Butcher's spies are in these woods. Their watchful, traitorous eyes are everywhere.

"You can't keep him here. If the Butcher finds out you're harboring the enemy, he'll kill you. After he rapes you. And tortures you for information." Jules' intense stare bore into her very soul. "We have to hide him in the woods."

Yvette adamantly shook her head and held her brother's feral gaze. "He can't run. He needs to lie still. In a clean bed." She squeezed Jules' calloused hand, tears filling her loving eyes. "He needs me. My skills as a healer. And my knowledge of herbs. Without proper treatment, he'll die of gangrene." She gently rinsed the soldier's matted hair, washing the blood and grime from his atrocious wound. "When he recovers, he'll want to rejoin his regiment. Until then, I'll keep him here with me." At the sound of the front door closing, she leaned forward to kiss her brother's scarred, bristled cheek. "And—having him with you would slow you down. Increase your risk of getting caught." She whispered into his proud, stubborn ear. "You joined *les Loups* to fight the Nazis. Let me do my part, too. This way, we can both avenge Papa, Jeffroi, and Jean-Michel."

Pierrick entered the room and held out two long, sturdy branches that formed a matched pair. "These will be the right length for crutches." He turned to Yvette. "Do you have wool to use as padding for under the shoulders?"

"Yes, I still have some that I haven't spun into yarn. It's dense, thick fleece. Perfect to cushion the top." Yvette finished cleansing the filthy wound on the soldier's damaged leg and rinsed away the soapy grime. "He's clean now. Let's get him out. Careful of his leg." She stepped back, keeping her hands on either side of the soldier's head to stabilize it, as each of the four men supported a limb and lifted the American out of the tub. Yvette quickly dried him off with a clean towel. "Please sit him upright on the edge of the bed so I can bandage his head wound. Then we'll lay him down so I can splint and stitch his broken leg."

While the men complied, Yvette fetched a clean shirt, cotton underwear, and long pants from the bedroom armoire where Yanna had kept her son's personal items. *She never could part with Cadec's things. They kept his memory alive for her. And now, I'm truly grateful that she did.*

Folding the clothing over her arm, Yvette retrieved her bag of herbs, a bottle of cognac, a needle and thread, a jar of lanolin, and several bunches of soft, raw wool. She laid the clothing beside the unconscious soldier, placed a towel on the bed, and tore some cotton fabric into long strips to use with the splint. While the men held the soldier still and Jules supported his head, Yvette applied some herbal salve that she'd made from calendula, rosemary, and raw honey to the wound at the base of his skull. She placed a soft cotton compress over the swelling and wrapped the injury with strips of cotton as bandages.

"Jules, lower his head onto the pillow as we lay him down." While her brother and Briac eased the American onto his back, Pierrick lifted the soldier's right leg and Yvette raised the damaged left, setting it upon the towel she'd placed over the bedspread.

"Hold him still while I set the leg," Yvette told the four *Loups* as she pulled the broken bone back into place. She aligned the ankle and foot, rubbing her homemade yarrow and comfrey ointment over the wound. "This will prevent bleeding and help the bone heal quickly," she informed the watchful, fascinated men.

After soaking the needle and thread in cognac, Yvette meticulously stitched the torn flesh over his broken bone. Wrapping soft cotton around the leg and ankle, she secured the fracture firmly in place. "When I put the wool against his leg, hold the splint so I can wrap bandages all around it like a cast." Yvette placed the soft wool padding on either side of the soldier's leg. While Jules and Pierrick held two sticks in place, she wrapped cotton strips around the entire splinted leg, ankle, and foot to form a makeshift cast. "I'll need to change the inner dressing on his wound twice a day to prevent infection. And the outer splint will keep the bone securely in place."

Yvette gestured to the clothing on the bed. "Let's dress him in these. They used to belong to Yanna's son Cadec." She helped Pierrick slip the soldier's sinewy arms into a cotton shirt, buttoning up the front. Carefully sliding first the underwear and then the pants over his injured leg, she and Pierrick finished dressing the wounded American. "We'll fold up the bottom of the loose pant leg to accommodate the splint."

Their task complete, she exhaled with satisfaction and relief. "Now, we let him sleep. When he wakes, I'll get him to drink some water infused with herbs to prevent infection." Yvette collected the soldier's torn, filthy uniform. "I'll wash and mend this—and hang it to dry inside the house so it won't be seen. I'll hide it with his boots and backpack in the storage area of the cellar—under the bed."

The four *Loups* left the sleeping soldier and exited the bedroom. Jules and Briac lugged the tub into the kitchen, carried it down the steps into the backyard, and dumped the filthy water at the edge of the woods. While Jules carried the empty tub back into the kitchen, Briac pumped several buckets of fresh water and brought them into the cottage.

With a nod of her head, Yvette indicated the empty tub. "Bring that into my bedroom and pour the water in. Fetch a couple more buckets so you can wash. I know you rarely get the chance to bathe because you live like hermits in the woods." She grinned at the dirty, scraggly men she dearly loved. "You four, take turns washing up. Leave your dirty clothes for me to mend and launder. I'll lay out four clean shirts and pants on the bed in my room. Pick up a set of clean clothing to put on after your bath. Then, come back here to the kitchen and eat your fill before you go."

The white cotton curtains with tiny blue wildflowers fluttered in the briny breeze, the tangy scent of the sea wafting in through the small window over the porcelain sink. Yvette set plates, napkins, and silverware on the table, pouring mugs of mint-infused water for each of the four *Loups*. She dumped the oysters from her satchel onto a huge platter and set it on the table before the ravenous men. "While you eat these as an appetizer, I'll fix you a quick meal. Steamed scallops, clams, and mussels that I harvested this morning." She flashed the famished *Loups* a sisterly smile. "There's a loaf of bread from Monsieur Dubois, some *brebis* cheese and sheep's milk from Monsieur Blanchard, and fresh strawberries from my plants behind the cottage. Come...*à table*!" With loving hands and a generous heart, Yvette seated her brother and three closest friends at the round oak table in her cheerful kitchen.

The starving men greedily pounced on the shellfish, their hunting knives slicing open the mollusks, slurping the delicious morsels with appreciative moans of delight.

Jules' dark eyes blazed with gratitude. In their profound depths, Yvette glimpsed the realization that he understood. This food had been meant to last her for several days. And she'd sacrificed it all for them. *Les Loups*. Her wolf brothers. She held his devoted gaze, her spirit soaring on the salty summer breeze.

Sublimely content, she set a pot of water to boil on

her small stove, fetched a few more buckets from the well, and—making several trips to carry them into the bedroom—finished filling the large tin tub. Yvette returned to the kitchen and leaned down to kiss Jules' rough cheek. "The bath is ready. Who's first?"

Pierrick rose from the table, wiping his gruff, grinning face. "*Moi.*" He pulled Yvette into his brawny arms and roughly kissed her cheek. His deep, husky voice was hoarse. "Thank you, Yvette. You're a sister to us all. What would *les Loups* do without you?"

She chuckled at the famished oyster eaters whose eyes shone with profound gratitude. Her overflowing heat soared on the soft wings of a sparrow.

Yvette escorted the brawny Pierrick into her chamber and the awaiting tub. She slipped quietly into the adjacent bedroom where the American soldier lay peacefully sleeping and fetched clean clothing from the armoire. Bringing four shirts and pants back into her own bedroom, she laid them upon her bed and spoke softly to the grubby, grimy brute. "Bathe and dress here in my room." She put a large basket on the floor. "Put your dirty clothing in this, for me to wash. And come back to the kitchen and join us when you're done." With a warm smile, Yvette left and returned to feed the famished *Loups*.

The water in the pot on the stove was boiling, so Yvette added the shellfish. While the seafood simmered, she placed the round loaf of *pain de campagne*, a large wedge of *brebis* sheep cheese, and fresh strawberries in the center of the table.

Wet, sandy-brown hair slicked back from his clean-shaven face, a glowing Pierrick rejoined them, and Briac rose from the table to take his turn in the tub.

Dark brown eyes glistened in his pale, gaunt visage. "I'll dump the dirty water and fetch a few buckets for Gwilherm and Jules." He bent down to kiss Yvette's cheek. "Thank you for taking such good care of us." His lopsided grin revealed a broken front tooth, a visible reminder of the harrowing encounter and narrow escape from one of the Butcher's barbaric *miliciens*.

Yvette hugged her brother's closest friend. "You're welcome. Now, wash quickly—so the seafood will still be hot when you're done."

She cleared away the platters of empty oyster shells, returning with steaming bowls of scallops, mussels, and clams. "We have butter made from Monsieur Blanchard's sheep milk. Delicious with fresh seafood."

The *Loups* dug into the crustaceans, licking their fingers and groaning with delight. The blissful contentment on their haggard faces and the thankful, shimmering eyes which held her gaze filled Yvette's empty soul.

The Nazis killed two of my blood brothers. But now, I have three more. Brothers of my heart. Les Loups.

When the men had all finished eating, and had bathed and dressed in clean clothing, Yvette kissed them goodbye and spoke quietly to Jules near the front door. "I need to go to the cove for more shellfish Friday morning. And I must go into town for supplies. Can you please come stay with the American while I'm gone? Even if he regains consciousness—which I surely hope he does soon—I still don't want to leave him alone. Could you come here Friday at dawn?" She searched her brother's wary eyes, glimpsing in them acknowledgement of the shared danger they all faced.

For *les Loups,* the constant risk of being caught by

la Milice.

For the American, the harrowing threat of Nazis who were undoubtedly searching for survivors of the plane crash.

And for Yvette, the inevitable encounter in the village with Étienne Boucher. The Butcher who openly lusted after her. And made his ardent desire abundantly clear.

Grim acceptance dulled Jules' perceptive gaze. "*D'accord.* Agreed. Friday morning at dawn."

"I'll have your clothes washed and mended. And feed you another decent meal." She wrapped her arms around Jules' rangy shoulders and rested her head over his fierce Breton heart. "I love you, Jules." She gazed up into his dark lupine gaze. "Be careful. See you Friday."

He kissed her cheeks with *la bise* of farewell and held her tight. "I love you, too, *ma petite soeur*. My little sister. Until Friday. At dawn."

Yvette lingered in the doorway.

And watched her brother—the wild alpha wolf—disappear into the dark Breton woods.

Chapter 2

Haunted Eyes

He struggled to wake up. His eyelids were fused shut. His parched throat was on fire, his thirst overwhelming and primal. Pain wracked his entire body. But gentle, nimble fingers softly stroked his hair. Wrapped a bandage around his throbbing head. And laid him gently down upon a soft pillow. Summoning every ounce of sheer will, he forced his eyes open. And gasped at the ethereal beauty before him.

Wild mane of long black curls tied into a loose ponytail, an enigmatic young woman sat in a wooden chair at the foot of the bed where he now reclined on his back. Battling dizziness and nausea, he watched her cut and remove the bloodied bandages from a hideous wound on the lower half of his left leg. She applied a soothing salve which instantly iced the fierce, burning pain. A hoarse moan of relief escaped his dry, cracked lips.

"*Bonjour.* Good morning." Her lilting voice flowed over him like a clear, limpid stream. She pulled her chair up to his side, slid a hand under his head to lift it, and held a glass of water to his desiccated mouth. "I'm glad you're awake. *Buvez un peu.* Drink a little."

He took a grateful swallow, desperate for more, but

she withdrew the glass and placed it upon the nightstand beside the bed. He searched her exquisitely beautiful—yet drawn, haggard face. Her haunted blue eyes, bleak as a wintry sky, were so pale they appeared silver.

Bewitching. Beguiling. Bewildering.

"*Parlez-vous français?*" She wiped his brow and stubbled cheeks with a cool, damp cloth.

"*Oui*," he croaked. Her calming touch was sublime.

"That's good," she replied in French. "We'll be able to communicate." She reached for the glass beside the bed, raised his head, and held the rim to his withered lips. "I've added herbs to this water, which will help prevent infection. Drink another sip or two. But slowly." When he'd complied, she put the glass back on the table and gestured to the bandages wrapped around his skull. "You've had a serious head injury. It's very fortunate you were wearing a helmet." Moving her chair back to the foot of the bed, she resumed tending the wound on his leg. "This ointment will help mend the broken bone. And, since the fracture also punctured your skin, the salve will prevent gangrene." The comforting caress of her fingertips sent tingles of pleasure up his injured leg. His body stirred at her touch. *At least parts of me still function normally.*

"What is your name?" Her lyrical voice interrupted his sensual reverie. She placed a small bandage over the wound on his calf, some wool padding inside each of two wooden splints, and wrapped strips of cotton securely around the entire lower leg.

"I…don't know." He couldn't remember his name. He didn't understand where he was, nor why he was here. He had a vague recollection of sitting with huddled men amid loud explosions and claps of thunder and lightning. "I remember a group of soldiers. We were being transported. There were explosions…and a lightning storm. We were in the air."

"I found you tangled up in a parachute, hanging from a tree. You must have been on the plane that was shot down nearby. I think the wind blew you into the forest and slammed you against the trunk." The woman walked across the room and held up a helmet, a pair of brown leather boots with lacing up the front, and a soldier's khaki uniform. "This is what you were wearing when I found you. Do you recognize the insignia?" She brought the uniform closer for him to see.

On the left sleeve, an emblem with a curved dark blue heading and the word Airborne embroidered in white letters was centered over a red square patch with two capital letter A's inside a blue circle.

"No, I don't." He frowned in frustration. He glanced up at her, standing at the foot of his bed. "Where am I? And how did you get me down from the tree?"

She smiled softly, her nurturing presence calm and soothing. "You're in the coastal town of *Le Vivier-Sur-Mer*. In the northwestern region of France called *la Bretagne*—Brittany in English." She folded the uniform and laid it near the helmet and boots before returning to the chair beside his bed. "To get you down from the tree, I enlisted the help of several friends." Lifting his head carefully off the pillow, she helped him drink a few more sips of herb-infused water. "They got you into my bathtub so I could wash the blood from your hair and the dirt from your wounds. They also helped me set the broken bone, splint your leg, and dress you in clean clothes." Compassionate, silvery eyes searched his stubbled face. In their haunted depths, he glimpsed a veiled mirror of pain and suffering. "My name is Yvette Fleury. Since you can't remember yours—and you're quite handsome—I'll call you Beau." Her warm smile stirred his soul.

"I like that." He returned her smile and eyed the pitcher on the nightstand. "Could I please have more water?"

"Of course. But remember—slow sips. In a little while, if you're hungry, I'll fix an *omelette aux champignons.* Do you like mushrooms?"

"I'm not sure. But since I'm starved, I'll eat anything you have. And be most grateful for the food." He grinned at her. In a reverent, grateful voice, he murmured, "Thank you, Yvette. For everything."

"You're welcome." She squeezed his calloused hand. "I'm glad you regained consciousness. You were out for a full day." She helped him drink a few more sips of water. "I'm sure your memory will return as you recover. It's most likely caused by your head injury."

Her gentle fingers stroked his furrowed brow, easing the worry and assuaging the pain. "I'm going to collect the eggs for the *omelette* now. I have hens in a coop behind the cottage." Yvette gestured to the sunny window on the bedroom wall through which he glimpsed a grassy yard surrounded by dense, obscure forest. "I also have a small vegetable garden, so I'll harvest a few carrots and peas for dinner. Try to sleep for a little while." She set a bucket on the floor beside the bed. "Use this as a bedpan. And, if you need to use the toilet…" she said, indicating a chair with the inner seat removed and a large bucket centered underneath, "…let me know and I'll help you stand—very carefully—with these crutches." She pointed to a pair of long, whittled oak branches with pads of wool secured at the top. "My friends made them. As well as the toilet—from a broken chair that I was planning to reupholster. Since I must keep you hidden, it's much safer than having you use the outhouse." She regarded him with haunted silver eyes. "The day after tomorrow, I must go into town for supplies. You'll get to meet my brother Jules. He's coming here to stay here with you while I'm gone." She leaned forward, pushing a strand of hair from his forehead as she whispered into his ear. "*Dormez maintenant.* Sleep now. I'll be back to check on you in a little while."

When the bedroom door closed softly, Beau shut his eyes. And drifted off to blissful, restorative sleep.

****

Yvette released her trio of hens from the wooden shed and tossed a handful of corn on the grassy lawn enclosed by tall shrubs, fruit trees, and vines. While the chickens pecked at the corn and searched for insects, she collected the eggs from the henhouse and placed them in a cloth-lined bowl. *These will make a fine omelette aux champignons.* From the trunk of a nearby oak, she gathered the mushrooms and wrapped them in a towel, carrying her parcel to the herb garden where she added a few sprigs of rosemary, basil, and thyme. She picked a head of lettuce, unearthed four carrots, and harvested several pods of peas and two large vine-ripened tomatoes from their supportive stalks, placing all the vegetables into a straw basket.

Spotting the wild blueberries amongst the dense vegetation, she decided to pick some for a simple dessert to go with the *omelette*. As she gathered the fruit, she thought of the handsome American soldier sleeping inside the stone cottage.

It will take at least six weeks for his broken leg to mend. He won't be able to walk without the crutches until late July. When I go back inside, I'll help him stand. Move around a bit. And show him the secret storage area under the bed. Where he can hide if the Nazis—or the Butcher's spies—come hunting for him.

Yvette glanced around the backyard, immensely grateful for the dense, thick hedgerow which sheltered the cottage from view and provided food for sustenance. The apples wouldn't be ready to pick until the fall, but the wild plum tree was laden with ripe fruit. As she plucked the sweet green plums and placed them in a bucket, Yvette planned a delightful surprise for her wounded soldier. *I'll make a tarte aux mirabelles. I have flour and lard for the pastry shell. And honey to add to these wild plums. There's still some of the pain de campagne from Monsieur Dubois. And enough scallops for a meal. I'll steam those…and serve them with the carrots and peas. Beau needs lots of protein for his wounds to heal.*

A wave of desire flooded her at the memory of his sculpted body rippled with muscles and dark hair. She shivered deliciously at the thought of Beau's hardened body molded against hers.

Another sensuous chill slipped up her spine. Suppressing her sultry reverie with a private smile, Yvette returned to the vegetable garden and stacked the container of blueberries inside the bucket of wild plums. She put the bowl of eggs inside the basket of vegetables and tucked the towel-wrapped mushrooms and herbs on top. Sliding the straw handle over her elbow, she grabbed the small bucket of fruit with her other hand and carried her precious cargo into the cottage.

She laid the fruit and vegetables on the countertop, then peeked in on her patient through the bedroom door. He was still sleeping peacefully, so Yvette returned to the kitchen to make the *tarte aux mirabelles*. She couldn't wait to surprise him with the delicious wild plum tart.

She preheated the oven. Measured the flour, salt, lard, and water. Blended the pastry dough, flattening it with her rolling pin and shaping it inside the pan. She washed the wild plums in the sink and removed the pits, cutting the fruit into halves and placing them into pastry-lined pie tin. *Two tablespoons of honey. Et voilà!* She slid the wild plum tart inside the hot oven to bake.

After tidying up the kitchen, Yvette poured a *tisane* of burdock root infusion into a cup and returned to the bedroom to find Beau awake. His scarred, handsome face broke into a heart-melting grin when he spotted her in the doorway.

Yvette's knees nearly buckled under her blue cotton dress. "Did you sleep well?" She entered the room and set the cup of herbal tea down on the bedside table. Pouring a fresh glass of water, she helped him sit up to drink it. The back of his muscular neck was hard and covered with soft, dark hair. *Like the rest of him.* Yvette swallowed forcefully as an impossible surge of desire swept through her.

He drank several large gulps, wiping the corners of his mouth before dazzling her with another grateful smile. "I did indeed." He handed her the empty glass.

She returned his smile and gave him the cup of *tisane*. "Drink it all. The herbs will cleanse your blood and prevent infection." As he complied, she retrieved her herbal supplies and bandages from the top drawer of the dresser and placed them on the table beside his bed. "I need to change the dressing on your wounds. I'll fetch some soap and water and be right back."

Yvette set the bowl, washcloth, and soap on the table and carefully removed the bandages wrapped around Beau's head. *I'll need to burn these so there are no traces of a wounded soldier that the Nazis—or the Butcher's spies—might find.*

She gently washed the wound and applied the herbal antiseptic salve. "The injury is healing nicely. The swelling has gone down, and there is no sign of infection." As she bent over him, wrapping clean cotton bandages around his head, her senses stirred as she inhaled his earthy, musky scent.

"Something smells amazing. What are you cooking?" Beau sniffed the welcoming aroma emanating from the kitchen.

Something does indeed smell amazing. You, my handsome patient. Yvette smiled at his eager, stubbled face. *"Une tarte aux mirabelles.* A wild plum tart."

Now that she'd finished dressing his head wound, Yvette placed a towel under his injured leg and carefully cut away the strips of cotton serving as a cast with a pair of scissors. She meticulously cleansed the entire area and reapplied her curative comfrey ointment. "While you were sleeping, I picked the fruit from the tree in my backyard. *Tarte aux mirabelles* is one of my favorite pies. I hope you'll love it, too." She replaced the padding inside the wooden splints with soft, clean wool and rewrapped his fractured lower leg.

She swam in the depths of his intense blue gaze. "Let me help you sit up," she suggested encouragingly, sliding her arm behind Beau's back. His muscles were hard and lean, and she hovered just above his broad, brawny shoulder. Once again, the tangy masculine scent washed her in a wave of longing. "We'll swing your legs over the edge of the bed. Slowly. I'll lift the injured one. Don't put any weight on it yet."

They shifted his legs so that he now sat erect, examining his surroundings and cautiously moving his head to gaze around the room.

"How do you feel?" Yvette watched him guardedly, the gifted healer assessing her injured patient.

"Starved." He broke into a charming, disarming grin. His blue eyes sparkled in the midday sun streaming through the open window.

The wings of a small sparrow fluttered in Yvette's hopeful heart. "That's a very good sign." She eyed him judiciously. "Do you think you could stand?"

He nodded. "I do feel a bit light-headed. But I think it's from hunger." He grinned sheepishly. "And I do need to use the toilet."

Yvette fetched the crutches, assisting Beau as he placed them under his armpits. "I'll help you stand. Ease yourself up onto your good leg."

As Beau lifted himself from the bed, Yvette guided him, but with his impressive upper body strength, he didn't need her help. Balancing his weight on the crutches, he walked tentatively with his uninjured leg. "These are just the right length."

"I used my measuring tape to be sure. You have very long legs." Now that he was standing, she could truly appreciate his height. Yvette was tall, but he towered over her. Her stomach quivered under his intense, appreciative gaze. "Sit here on the makeshift toilet.

There's soft cloth on the arm of the chair. Just toss it in that bucket when you're done, and I'll wash it for reuse." She indicated a pitcher and basin on the bedside table. "There's soap, water, and a clean towel for you to use. In the meantime, I'll go prepare our *omelette aux champignons*. Call me if you need any help."

Yvette returned to the cozy blue and white kitchen, flustered by the undeniable, magnetic attraction that pulled her toward the wounded American soldier. *His eyes peer right into my soul. And his scent stirs my senses. I feel a deep, earthy connection to him. As if fate has bound us together…*

A few minutes later, he joined her in the kitchen, lowering himself onto a chair at the rectangular oak table, leaning his crutches against the adjacent empty seat. He sniffed the air appreciatively and flashed her an eager, boyish grin. "Mmm…smells fantastic."

Yvette lowered the heat and left the *omelettes* simmering on the stove. She set the remainder of the *pain de campagne* and some *brebis* cheese on the table in front of him. "This is made from the milk of my neighbor's sheep. It has a rich, nutty flavor. Spread it on the hearty bread. It's *delicious*."

As she arranged slices of ripe, beefy tomatoes over a bed of lettuce on each of two salad plates, she watched him from the corner of her eye. He obviously enjoyed the grainy bread and flavorful cheese from his enthusiastic chewing. She scattered some finely chopped fresh basil over the tomatoes and added her homemade garlic vinaigrette dressing. "The lettuce and tomatoes are from my garden." She proudly set the small plates on the table. "I just need to add the herbs and cheese to the *omelettes*. I'll be right back."

Yvette sprinkled a few sprigs of fresh rosemary and minced garlic over the *omelettes*, folding each one separately with a spatula. She grated some cheese to melt on top and slid them onto blue ceramic plates, which she carried to the table.

Placing the larger of the two mushroom, cheese, and herb omelets in front of Beau, she announced, "I made yours with four eggs. You need the extra protein to heal." With a warm smile, she poured two glasses of mint-infused water, set them near the plates, and sat down beside him.

Beau leaned over his omelet and inhaled the aroma. "Yvette, this is incredible." He took a bite and closed his eyes, savoring the mellow flavor as he swallowed appreciatively. "And it tastes even better than it looks."

Yvette's hot cheeks flushed with pride.

He devoured his omelet and salad, wiped his mouth on a cloth napkin, and leaned back in his chair with a contented sigh. "That was fantastic." Satiety and appreciation shone on his handsome, bruised face. "Thank you. For saving my life. Tending my wounds. Sheltering and feeding me. I'm profoundly grateful."

Yvette smiled at the alluring American as she rose from the table. "You're welcome, Beau." She crossed the kitchen, removed the *tarte aux mirabelles* from the oven, and placed it on the cooling rack. The delicious aroma of sweet fruit and baked pastry mingled with the pine scent of the forest and the briny tang of the nearby sea, floating through the open window.

She turned toward Beau. "Ever since the Nazi invasion of France, coffee has become very scarce. But I can offer you a cup of chicory." She poured two cups of the steaming beverage and carried them back to the table, setting one down in front of Beau. "Although it's not the same, the flavor is pleasant." Yvette sat back down beside him to savor the warm, licorice-like brew.

"Are you all alone? Do you have family nearby?" Beau's inquisitive gaze searched hers.

Yvette stared into her cup, the bitter memories floating like storm clouds in the dark, liquid depths. "Yes, I live here by myself."

She took a sip of the coffee substitute, clutching the cup for strength as she voiced the unspeakable horror. "The Gestapo slaughtered my entire family. All but one brother, Jules. He's the sole survivor of the Nazi attack."

Chicory spilled onto the tablecloth from her badly shaking hand. She lowered the cup to the saucer, whisking away her angry, bitter tears.

Tracing the rim of her cup with a fingertip, Yvette retraced the painful past.

"My family had a farm in the neighboring village of Cancale. I lived there with my parents, grandmother, and three brothers in a large house on a cliff overlooking the sea. We raised sheep, processed wool, and harvested vegetables to sell in the local market." Haunted by distant ghosts, she stared sightlessly at the thick trees in the backyard through the open kitchen window.

"Each spring, my father and brothers would shear the fleece from our herd of sheep. My mother and grandmother taught me to clean, card, comb, and spin the wool." She took a sip of chicory, gazing into her steaming cup. "I was twelve when *Maman* died, so my grandmother *Mamie* and I did all the cooking and cleaning while the men worked the fields, tended the crops, and cared for the animals."

Beau's blue eyes bore into her very soul.

"*Mamie* had a close friend, Yanna—a widow who lived alone in this cottage. My grandmother and I used to visit her often, and the two of them showed me how to gather shellfish in the nearby cove." Yvette smiled faintly at the fond memories. "After my grandmother died, I still visited Yanna frequently. She taught me the natural medicine of healing herbs. How to make ointments, salves, and tinctures. When she became too frail to harvest seafood, I would go to the shore alone and bring shellfish back for her. I still go to that same cove— that's where I collected the scallops that you and I will eat for tonight's meal. Twice a week, I go to that sheltered inlet for seafood." She held Beau's intense gaze. "Food is very scarce. Because the Nazis confiscate our supplies to feed the German army."

Beau repositioned the injured leg with his hands, shifting his weight in the chair. He scrutinized her with intelligence and incomprehension. "You mentioned the Nazis. The Gestapo who slaughtered your family. I don't understand. Germany invaded France?"

Yvette nodded, unwanted tears blurring her vision of his confused, concerned expression. "Four years ago. That's when they murdered my father and brothers. And commandeered our family farm."

She took a deep breath, summoning the courage to relive the nightmare.

"I had gone to the cove to harvest shellfish, and I was coming home from Yanna's." Yvette swallowed the huge lump in her constricted throat. "I stopped abruptly at the edge of the woods. Because four black sedans with swastika flags were parked in front of our farmhouse." She rose from the table on unsteady legs and walked toward the window, running her fingers back and forth on the countertop with anxious, nervous tension.

Turning toward Beau, she leaned against the ledge for support, gripping the edges tightly with both hands, bracing herself against the gruesome memory. Her stomach quivered and her mouth went bone dry. "While I stood hidden in the trees, watching in abject horror, they lined my father and brothers up on the opposite edge of the forest, near our farmhouse. And gunned them down. Right before my eyes."

She buried her face and sobbed into her shaking hands.

Beau bolted from his chair. He hobbled across the kitchen, leaned the crutches against the wall, and braced himself along the counter next to Yvette. A sinewy arm pulled her into a protective, sheltering embrace. He kissed the top of her head and wordlessly held her tight.

She melted into him, resting her head over his wildly thumping heart. The exposed dark hair of his broad chest brushed her cheek, his masculine scent both soothing and scintillating.

After a few moments, she raised her head to look up into his compassionate, expressive gaze. "I stumbled through the woods and came back here. To Yanna's cottage. She took me in. She knew at once that something terrible had happened." Yvette ran her fingers along Beau's chest, lightly touching the tuft of dark hair, resisting the urge to bury her nose in its comforting scent. "I was so traumatized by what I'd seen that I couldn't even speak. For weeks. Until the day my brother Jules showed up here. *Alive*."

Tears streamed down her face as she beamed up at Beau.

His calloused fingers traced her wet cheek and

stroked her long black curls.

"He'd somehow managed to crawl into the woods near the farmhouse. Where he was found by the French Resistance group called *Les Loups*. The Wolves. They removed the bullet from his chest. Luckily, it was up near the shoulder and not close to his heart. They cared for him for weeks until he recovered. And could come tell me that he'd miraculously survived."

She smothered her face in Beau's dampened shirt. "Jules is now the leader of *les Loups*. The alpha wolf. Relentlessly hunted by the Gestapo. And *la Milice*. The French collaborators who work for the Nazis."

Yvette crumbled as she looked up at Beau. "Their commander is Étienne Boucher, known as the Butcher for his atrocities. He tortures prisoners to obtain information. And he's scouring the woods for *les Loups*." Yvette's lips trembled under Beau's piercing blue gaze. "The Butcher must know about your plane being shot down. He'll be searching for survivors." She stroked the side of his stubbled cheek, her heart in her throat. "He'll be hunting *you*."

Beau curved his finger and lifted her chin. His mesmerizing gaze held hers as he lowered his full, sensuous mouth to softly brush her lips.

Yvette's knees weakened, her receptive body stirring at his tender touch. *No, Yvette. He hasn't even healed.*

She stepped away from the alluring American and his tempting, tantalizing kiss. "But there is a place for you to hide. Come, let me show you."

Leading him back into the bedroom where he'd been sleeping earlier, she pushed the bed aside and pointed to a circular knot in the grain of the pinewood floor. "See this nodule? Press on it, and the panel lifts." She demonstrated, dislodging a four-foot section of the floor to reveal an underground opening. "This is a separate, hidden storage area within the foundation of the cottage. It's not connected to the rest of the cellar, which is accessible through a trapdoor near the front entrance."

Beau peered into the cavernous area below the bed as Yvette gathered his uniform, boots, and knapsack from the corner of the room.

"I washed and repaired your uniform while you were unconscious. I'll store your military items down here for you to retrieve when you need them." She zipped the army uniform inside the backpack and laid it on the floor at the edge of the opening. Lowering herself through the hole, she stood on the earthy ground below and looked up at Beau. "Hand me the boots first, then the knapsack."

He complied and watched through the floor aperture as she laid them against the stone wall of the subterranean foundation. "This area is approximately three meters square, so you can stand and move around a bit." She pointed to the side rear wall. "There's an enormous support column, with another concealed area behind it. If anyone peers down into this hole, you can hide back there."

She assessed Beau, hovering near the opening above her. "Can you balance on one leg and give me a hand? I'll need help pulling myself back up."

He leaned against the wall to brace himself, shifting his weight onto his good leg, and lifted Yvette up through the hole.

"Thank you," she said, brushing the dirt from her dress and hands. She replaced the panel in the floor and covered it with the bed. "If anyone ever comes to the door, wait for the signal. One knock, followed by three, then one more. If you don't hear that exact pattern, then you must hide in the cellar. Lower your crutches first, then your body. Balance yourself on your good leg and replace the panel securely in the floor. Hide your things—and yourself—behind the thick column. If anyone searches the cottage, you'll be well concealed down there."

Beau leaned his crutches against the wall and sat on the edge of the bed. His brow furrowed with worry. "If the Nazis find me, they'll execute you for sheltering me. I can't stay here. I can't risk your life, Yvette."

She plopped down beside him and took both of his large, rough hands in hers. Her thumb stroked the hair covering his large knuckles. "I'm a healer, and you're my patient. I will keep you here until you've fully recovered. If anyone comes, you'll hide in the cellar." She kissed his scarred, calloused hand. "I'm a member of the French Resistance. One of *les Loups*, just like my brother Jules." Ferocity and fury burned in her heart as she held his fiery gaze. "The Nazis murdered my father and two of my brothers. And I will avenge them. *By healing you.*"

Resolute, Yvette stood and stared confidently at him. "And now, my stubborn patient, you must rest." She helped Beau recline on the pillow, lifting his injured leg onto the bed and securing it under the blanket. Pulling the covers up around him, she leaned down to tuck him in.

Beau wrapped his arms around her neck, pulling her toward him as his full, eager mouth found hers. The tip of his tongue deliciously outlined the silky lining of her slightly parted lips.

Warmth flooded her body and settled between her thighs. *I want him. Badly. But in six short weeks, he'll be gone. I can't lose my heart. No matter how handsome and alluring he is.* Yvette delicately withdrew from his enticing embrace. "For dinner tonight," she said, collecting her wits and smoothing the sides of her dress, "we'll have steamed scallops, with fresh vegetables from the garden. And the *tarte aux mirabelles* for dessert." She stared into his inviting gaze, suppressing the impossible desire to lay down at his side and welcome his amorous advances. "*Dormez bien*, Beau. Sleep well."

With a reluctant smile and a resigned sigh, he closed his beautiful eyes.

Yvette collected the chamber pot to empty in the outhouse. Slipping quietly from the peaceful room, she softly closed the bedroom door.

Chapter 3

Dangerous Rumors

Yvette breathed a sigh of relief at the familiar pattern of knocks on the front door indicating that Jules had arrived safely. It was still dark, so it was unlikely that he had been seen, but the ever-present threat of capture grated her already frazzled nerves. She opened the door and whisked her brother safely into the cottage.

"Beau is still asleep," she whispered as she kissed his two cheeks in greeting and led him into the kitchen where a lamp illuminated the gloom. She poured Jules a cup of chicory and seated him at the table. "When he wakes up, fix an omelet for each of you. There are six eggs, some mushrooms, a wedge of *brebis* cheese, half a loaf of bread, and a bowl of fresh strawberries that I picked yesterday." She downed the rest of her brew and rinsed the cup in the sink. "I'm off to the cove to harvest shellfish, then I'm stopping by Monsieur Dubois' cottage for bread, corn, and oats. Jacques Blanchard said last week that he'd have three bags of wool for me today. It was all he could manage to set aside."

Since Jacques and his granddaughter Lola raised sheep, they were forced each spring during the shearing season to process the wool, make blankets for the Nazis, and deliver them to the Butcher's men in town. Jacques gave Yvette as much wool as he could spare, for her to spin into yarn and knit scarves, gloves, and sweaters for *les Loups.* Extremely dangerous for both of them, for if they were caught, they'd be executed for stealing supplies destined for the Wehrmacht army.

Yvette buttoned her jacket and donned her gloves. "I'll come back here to put our seafood in the icebox and hide the bags of wool before I head into town. Since I need to get a slab of ice for the refrigerator, some coal for the stove, and several other supplies, Monsieur Dubois is hitching his mule to the wagon for me to take into the village today." She picked up her rubber boots and leaned down to kiss Jules goodbye. "Don't leave the cottage for any reason. And if anyone comes to the door, you and Beau hide in the cellar under the bed. Promise?" She searched his eagle eyes, dark as bitter coffee. She knew he'd rather die fighting than hide like a coward. But she also knew he wanted to live. For Lola. The woman he loved with every beat of his fierce Breton heart.

"Promise." He stood and wrapped his arms around her. "You be careful, too, *ma petite soeur.*"

With a warm hug, Yvette left her beloved brother and her sleeping soldier in the small stone cottage. And trekked through the woods to fetch the mule, Suzette.

Marcel Dubois had her saddled and ready to go when Yvette arrived at his cottage in the early predawn light. "*Merci, Monsieur,*" she said gratefully as she climbed into the saddle. "I'll be back in a couple hours with a nice harvest of shellfish for you."

"Splendid. When you return, I'll load the flour, corn, and oats into the wagon and hitch it up for your trip into town. See you soon. *À bientôt, Madmoiselle.*" The stout, bald baker went back into his cottage as Yvette rode through the dense woods to the sheltered cove on the seashore.

Two hours later, she loaded the heavy satchels of scallops, mussels, oysters, and clams onto the mule's pack and rode back to the cozy house in the forest. "*Bonjour, Madame Dubois,*" Yvette said to the plump baker's wife who came down the steps to greet her. "I have some delicious mussels and clams for you today. They'll be tender, succulent, and sweet." Yvette dismounted and unpacked the satchel, pouring the contents into the basket that Marie-Claire Dubois set on the ground before her.

"*Merci*, Yvette. Would you like to come in for a cup of chicory while Marcel hitches up the wagon?" Marie-Claire wiped her hands on the apron which covered the front of her dress.

"Yes, that would be lovely. But I can't stay long. I need to fetch ice to refrigerate my seafood." Yvette carried the basket of shellfish up the front stairs and into the cottage as Marcel Dubois emerged from the stables, pulling the wheeled wooden wagon toward the mule.

The interior layout of the baker's cottage was much like Yvette's. The front foyer opened onto a living room with a large fireplace on the left wall and a perpendicular rustic kitchen across the back. A narrow hall extended from the entrance to two bedrooms on the right. Madame Dubois led Yvette into the kitchen where a large pot of savory stew simmered on the stove.

"Mmm. Something smells delicious." Yvette placed the basket of shellfish on the wooden kitchen table.

"Bean soup. I purchased a ham hock for the broth with my ration coupon. I was lucky indeed." Marie-

Claire separated the mussels and clams into two separate bowls and placed them into her icebox. "I'll serve the clams tonight and steam the mussels tomorrow. Thank you, Yvette. Marcel and I are grateful for the seafood you provide." She poured two cups of chicory, handed one to Yvette, and sat down with her at the table. Her small, dark eyes gleamed in the morning sunlight.

Yvette had the disturbing sensation of staring into the beady orbs of a weasel. "And I am thankful for your bread, flour, and grains. My hens are laying well, because of the corn you give me." Yvette sipped the chicory, savoring the slightly bitter licorice flavor. She idly wondered what malicious gossip Marie-Claire Dubois seemed so anxious to share.

"As you know, everyone in the village comes into the bakery for bread. And Marcel hears all the rumors." Marie-Claire leaned across the table toward Yvette, breathless with excitement, positively salivating with salacious news. "The Butcher's men found two American soldiers! Survivors of the plane that was shot down a few days ago." She sipped her chicory, eyeing Yvette over the rim of her cup. "Apparently, they talked, before dying under torture. It seems their leader—who jumped from the burning plane—was blown off course. *Into our forest.*"

Yvette's stomach dropped to the floor. She veiled her shock with a calming swallow of chicory. *I can't let Marie-Claire see the fear and guilt in my eyes. She'll go to the Butcher with her suspicions. And turn me in for a slab of roast beef.* Inhaling to regain her composure, she replied with feigned indignation. "Imagine that! An American soldier in our very own Breton woods."

"The Butcher announced that his men are scouring

the forest, searching for him. One way or another—whether dead or alive—they'll find him. *La Milice* never fails." The wrinkles around Marie-Claire's thin lips puckered into a snide, smug smile.

"Yes, I'm sure you're right." Yvette finished her cup of chicory and rose from the table on quavering legs. "Thank you for the hospitality. I really must get going now. I hope you have a lovely day. And enjoy your hearty bean soup. *Bonne journée, Madame Dubois.*" Yvette ducked her chin graciously, left the kitchen, and exited the cottage.

Her pulse hammered wildly in her tightly constricted throat.

"I've placed the sacks of flour, corn, and oats here in the wagon. Along with a hearty loaf of *pain de campagne*, which I wrapped in a cloth to keep clean." Marcel Dubois, the doddering bald baker, handed the mule's reins to Yvette.

"*Merci, Monsieur.* I'll return the carriage later this afternoon when I come back from the village. Thank you again for lending it to me. I'll see you soon." Yvette hoisted herself into the mule's saddle and, trailing the harnessed wagon behind her, headed off along the wooded path toward Jacques Blanchard's cabin.

"*Bonjour, Yvette!* How are you today, my dear?" His scruffy beard as white as his long, thick hair, the gruff but generous sheep farmer grinned from ear to ear.

"*Bonjour, Jacques.* I'm fine, thank you. I have some lovely scallops and oysters for you today." Yvette dismounted, kissed her kind neighbor's two wrinkled cheeks, and unloaded the satchel of seafood from the back of the wagon.

"Lola is inside, in the kitchen. Why don't you bring

the seafood in to her while I hide the bags of wool in the carriage? I also have a wheel of *brebis* cheese and three bottles of sheep's milk for you as well." Jacques warmly kissed Yvette's hand, a merry twinkle in his caring, crinkled gaze.

"Thank you, Jacques. I'll bring this to Lola." Yvette carried the satchel up the stairs and into the cozy wooden cabin with thatched straw roof.

In the large kitchen, wooden walls painted white created an airy, welcoming ambiance. Red and white floral curtains fluttered in the early summer breeze over two open windows above the porcelain sink where Lola washed dishes and smiled as Yvette entered the room. "*Bonjour, Yvette!*" Waves of chestnut curls tumbling to her petite shoulders, the dimple in her left cheek highlighted the sparkle in Lola's golden-brown eyes. She hastily dried her soapy hands and rushed to greet Yvette with *la bise* of fond greeting.

"I've brought some oysters and scallops today. Your grandfather told me to bring them to you." Yvette returned the affectionate hug and placed the canvas satchel on the oak table, opening it for Lola to see the contents inside.

"Ooh, wonderful! I'll make a seafood feast tonight. It will be delicious. Thank you so much." Lola poured the seafood into a large bowl and placed it inside the icebox.

Her pretty face crumpled as she turned toward Yvette and grasped both her hands. Desperation shone in her distraught gaze. "Have you seen Jules?"

I can't tell her Jules is at my cottage. She would run right to him. And discover that I'm hiding an American soldier. I hate to lie to her. But no one can know about

42

Beau. Not even Lola or Jacques. Because, under torture, everyone talks.

"No…I haven't seen him. I hope he's all right." Yvette swallowed a huge lump of guilt as Lola's limpid eyes filled with unshed tears.

"When you do see him," she choked, "please tell Jules how much I love him. That I can't wait for this bloody war to end." Lola squeezed Yvette's hands, her impassioned voice imploring. "Tell him he has to *stay alive*…so he and I can be married."

Yvette comforted the overwrought friend who would one day—God willing—become her sister-in-law. "I will, Lola. I promise."

After a few moments, Lola raised her blotchy face from Yvette's shoulder, wiped her swollen eyes, and smiled bravely. "I'm glad I got to see you today."

"Me, too. But I must leave now. I have to go into town for supplies. Pray that I won't run into the Butcher." Yvette kissed Lola's cheeks as she bid her farewell. "Bye for now. See you soon. Take good care of your dear *Papi*."

With a forced, courageous smile, Lola nodded and reluctantly returned to washing dishes.

Yvette went outside to find Jacques Blanchard concealing three bags of wool under blankets in the flat wooden wagon among the sacks of flour, oats, and corn that the baker Monsieur Dubois had given her.

"You're all set now. Cheese, milk, wool, and some lanolin for your herbal ointments." The wiry old man cautiously approached Yvette, his amiable expression becoming somber. His stern voice wavered with warning. "There's talk in town of the Butcher's men scouring these woods. Looking for survivors of the plane

43

that the Germans shot down." His warm, calloused hands enveloped Yvette's cold fingers. "Tell Jules the *Loups* need to relocate. *La Milice* is not just searching for American soldiers. They're swarming the forest, hunting members of the French Resistance. It's much too dangerous for the *Loups* to remain here."

Jules won't leave these Breton woods. He and the Loups want to find the survivors of the plane crash, too. And aid the Allies in sabotaging the Germans at every possible turn. Even if I warn him, Jules won't listen. He's much too stubborn. Just like Papa used to be.

Yvette gazed into Jacques Blanchard's shrewd, compassionate gaze. He'd lost his son and daughter-in-law—Lola's parents—when the Germans bombed Paris in June 1940. The same month and year that the Nazis gunned down Yvette's father and two brothers. The shared loss was a strong bond between Yvette and Jacques Blanchard. And the fact that Lola and Jules were head over heels in love further strengthened their familial ties. "I'll tell him. If I see him. Thank you, Jacques. I'll be back on Wednesday with more seafood."

After an emotional hug goodbye, Yvette climbed into the saddle and directed the mule-drawn wagon back to her cottage in the dense Breton woods.

With the distinct pattern of knocks, she signaled her arrival to Jules and Beau. Unlocking the front door with her key, she carried the seafood into the kitchen where the two men were finishing up their *omelettes aux champignons* and munching on fresh strawberries. Yvette hoisted the two satchels onto the countertop and poured out the seafood. "I'm glad to see you're both eating." She walked over to the table, kissed Jules on each cheek, and smiled at Beau. "I'll change your bandages before I head into town. And when I come back later, I'll fix us all a lovely seafood feast."

She went out to the wagon, brought the bags of wool into the kitchen, and set them on the floor in the back of the room. Returning to the counter, she separated the seafood to store in the icebox.

Yvette glanced uneasily at her brother seated at the oak table. "You must stay here until dark. Madame Dubois and Jacques Blanchard both informed me of rumors circulating in town. The Butcher's men found two Americans. They're scouring the woods, searching for more survivors of the plane that was shot down." Her voice croaked in her parched throat. "And they're not just hunting for American soldiers. They're also tracking *les Loups*."

Jules averted his glowering gaze and popped a ripe strawberry into his taut mouth.

"Lola wanted me to tell you how much she loves you." Yvette's gentle fingers brushed her brother's dark hair from his bitter, scornful frown. "She also begs you to *stay alive*. So that the two of you can marry when this wretched war is over."

Anguish blazed across his scowling, impassioned face.

His love for Lola will keep him alive. I must believe that with every fiber of my being. She cradled her brother's beloved head against her chest and kissed his dark, shaggy locks. *Jules is all that's left of my entire family. I can't lose him, too.*

"You say the Butcher's men found two American soldiers? Do you know if they're still alive?" Beau's voice was laced with frantic tension. He undoubtedly hoped the prisoners had been on the same plane as his. If they were part of his regiment, they would know his identity. And his urgent military mission. The reason he'd been flown into France.

Yvette stared at her feet and gulped. "I'm sorry to say that the soldiers are both dead. The Butcher's men tortured them for information." Fear gripped her heart at the despair in Beau's bleak gaze. "*La Milice* knows about you. It seems the Americans revealed that their leader— a parachutist—was blown off course by the heavy winds. Right into these Breton woods." She walked over to him and rested her hand on his broad shoulder. "We must be extra cautious. Don't leave the cottage for any reason. And we'll keep the bedroom curtains closed."

At his nod of acceptance, Yvette fetched clean bandages, herbal supplies, and healing ointment. She returned to Beau's side and carefully removed the cotton strips wrapped around his head.

"The wound is healing nicely. Another day or two, and we can leave it uncovered." She washed the injury, applied the antiseptic salve, and rewrapped his head with soft, clean cloth. "Let's take a look at your leg."

She lifted the lower leg onto an empty chair and cut away the strips binding the splints. Removing the soiled bandage, she inspected the skin underneath. "Excellent. No sign of infection. It will take another five or six weeks for the bone to mend. But, when I leave your head wound unwrapped, I'll leave this skin exposed as well. The air can help both injuries heal more quickly." She cleansed the stitches, applied the herbal ointment, replaced the padding inside the splints with clean wool. And rewrapped Beau's broken leg in the makeshift cast.

Tossing the bloodied remnants into the fire inside her stove, Yvette tidied up the kitchen and washed her hands in the sink. "Let's get you back into bed to rest," she said to Beau. "You need as much sleep as possible to recover from your injuries. Jules is here to help if you need him. I'll be back from the village in two or three hours."

Beau's stubbled cheeks broke into a grateful grin. "Thank you, Yvette. With a full stomach, I could definitely sleep for a while." He arose from the chair and leaned down to plant a soft kiss on her cheek. "See you when you get back." Crutches under his arms, Beau withdrew from the kitchen and hobbled toward the bedroom for a much-needed nap.

"Well, I'm off to get supplies. Stay inside and keep hidden. Promise?" She kissed her brother's scarred cheek and clutched him tightly.

"Promise," he whispered in her ear and hugged her in return. "And you be careful, too, *ma petite soeur*. Beware the bloody butcher."

With a frisson of dread, Yvette said goodbye to her brother and locked the cottage door behind her. Atop the loyal mule Suzette pulling the flat wagon, she plodded along the dirt path through the forest into town.

Chapter 4

The Relentless Hunter

In the local supply store, apprehensive villagers redeemed their ration coupons for scarce commodities such as sugar, cheese, milk, and bread. Étienne Boucher scrutinized every transaction while four of his armed *miliciens* stood, rifle in hand, ready to seize anyone suspected of fraud. He loved having this power over them all. It made him feel like a god.

The terror in their eyes thrilled him, the stench of their fear exhilarating. The local French women—whose husbands languished in forced labor camps, working themselves to death for the Nazi regime while their neglected wives and children starved at home—would spread their skinny, weakened legs and let him slake his insatiable lust in exchange for a cut of beef, a ham shank, or even a simple bag of rare coffee. God, he loved being the Section Leader of the local *Milice*. The highest-ranking member of *les collabos*—the French who collaborated with the Gestapo.

He, Étienne Boucher, was the most powerful man in *le Vivier-Sur-Mer*.

As he stood behind the counter next to the trembling shopkeeper, Étienne spotted Yvette Fleury enter the store and take her place in line. Wild black mane cascading down her slim back, pale blue gaze shrouded in mystery, she exuded an irresistible savage aura that he longed to tame in the same way he broke his fiery, spirited horses.

Ride them mercilessly until they submitted to his superior, indomitable will.

Or died in stubborn, futile resistance.

The superstitious townspeople of *le Vivier-Sur-Mer* believed the age-old legends of enchanted woods haunted by fairies, dwarves, and shapeshifting wolves. Convinced that she possessed otherworldly magic, everyone feared Yvette Fleury, calling her *the Witch of the Breton Woods*, for she had curiously appeared four years ago, when the Nazis had first invaded France. Living like a recluse in the darkest heart of the forest with the old wise woman Yanna, Yvette had learned how to concoct peculiar potions, elixirs, herbal tinctures and tonics. Her pale, silvery eyes seemed haunted. Mysterious. Bewitching. As a result, none of the young men in the village dared court her, and no one ventured near her cottage for fear of evil enchantment.

Yet—unlike the villagers who recoiled from her in fear—Étienne Boucher was irresistibly drawn to Yvette Fleury.

Like a moth to a flickering flame.

"*Bonjour, Yvette*," he drawled, slithering up beside her as she waited nervously in line. "Haven't seen you for quite a while. What supplies have you come for today?"

Her full lips quivered into a forced, feigned smile. "*Bonjour, Monsieur Boucher.* I need a block of ice for my refrigerator. Some coal for my stove. And a few other items, like soap and fabric. For a new dress."

He sidled up to her, subtly inhaling the delicate rose

fragrance of her luxurious, abundant tresses. His body thickened as his ravenous gaze roved over her full breasts, trim waist, and rounded hips. He longed to thrust his steely sword into her slick, tight sheath. "I could provide you with all that and much more." He breathed heavily into her ear, yearning to suckle the tender flesh along her slender neck. "Prime cuts of roast beef or ham. Real coffee…cognac…champagne…chocolate. Whatever you desire. Just say the word, and I'll bring them personally to your cottage in the woods." He brushed his lips against her soft hair, his hardened body throbbing with need. "Where you can show me…your *gratitude.*"

She stepped away from him and lowered her eyes to the rations coupon book tightly clenched in her trembling hand. "Thank you for the generous offer, *Monsieur,* but I must politely decline. Excuse me. It is my turn in line." Yvette stumbled to the counter and presented her ration coupons to the shopkeeper, who summoned a teenaged boy to load the items into the wagon hitched outside the shop.

"An enemy plane was shot down a few days ago." Étienne hovered near Yvette but addressed the dozen or so townspeople anxiously waiting in line. "My men captured two American prisoners." He scowled at the cowering crowd. "Under torture, they revealed that their commanding officer had been blown by parachute into these woods." His deep voice rumbled with potent fury as he scrutinized the petrified villagers. "Anyone with information regarding his whereabouts is required by law to inform *la Milice.* Failure to do so will result in execution." Brows furrowed menacingly, Étienne reveled in the exquisite terror on their frightened faces.

"And anyone harboring a fugitive will die a slow, agonizing death."

An armed member of *la Milice*—clad in the distinctive blue uniform, brown shirt, and blue beret—burst through the door, gasping for breath. "Étienne—we've captured one of *les Loups*! Come quickly. They're making him talk." The panting soldier grinned in wicked delight, a gruesome gleam in his greedy black gaze.

Adrenaline surged in Étienne's veins. He'd torture the bloody bastard, learn the name of the leader of *les Loups,* and discover the location of their hideout in the Breton woods. And then—to ease his unbridled lust for Yvette Fleury—he'd stop by to visit Mireille Garnier. With her husband gone for two years now, she was most appreciative of his gifts of black-market goods. For a bag of sugar, she'd crouch on all fours like a bitch in heat. And let him mount her like a rutting stag. Hard as a rock at the lurid image, he adjusted his swollen shaft.

And dashed with Bruno out the front door of the supply shop.

****

The slaughterhouse—with its huge metal hooks, chains, clamps, and enormous vats to haul away blood and gore—was the perfect place to torture prisoners. As Étienne entered the dimly lit wooden building behind the local butcher shop, the revolting odor of vomit, blood, piss, and shit assailed his seasoned nostrils.

A naked prisoner, his mauled body shredded in long, garish slices like a carcass of beef, hung suspended by his arms from a metal hook in the ceiling. Splotches of hair had been yanked from his bloodied scalp, his head lolling forward onto a bruised, battered torso. Swollen eyes were fused shut, his disfigured face a hideous blend of black and blue. Blood and feces trailed down the prisoner's splayed hairy legs, secured by ropes attached to metal loops hammered into the earthen floor. The carved flesh of his limbs had been flayed and spliced, exposing shattered, splintered, bloodied bones.

"He's dead. But he told us *les Loups* live in the woods near a hidden limestone cave. About four miles southwest of the village." Didier, one of Étienne's most trusted *miliciens,* wiped the dark blood from the serrated edges of his jagged hunting knife.

"Did you get the name of their leader?" Étienne's heart hammered in his taut chest, his sweaty palms clenched into tight fists. His heaving breath hitched in unbearable anticipation.

"Code name *Garou.* Werewolf. This sorry bastard didn't know the real name. He would've told us if he did. We crushed his fucking balls with these." Sylvain, a brawny, beastly member of *la Milice,* showed Étienne a grisly pair of hair-encrusted, bloody pliers. A gruesome grin distorted Sylvain's scarred, brutal face.

Étienne scoffed in disgust. *Garou. Named after the alpha wolf of La Tribu des Loups—the legendary shapeshifting Wolf Tribe in the enchanted Forest of Brocéliande. Birthplace of the wizard Merlin and the infamous Morgan la Fée. Ridiculous, superstitious Breton myths. Fucking fairy tales.* "Search the woods surrounding the cave. That's their den. Bring me the alpha wolf. I want this *Garou.*"

"*À vos orders, Monsieur.* I'll send my men right away." Didier saluted Étienne, turned abruptly on his booted heels, and exited the slaughterhouse to obey.

"Hang the body in town. Near the supply store. I want everyone to see what we do to traitors." Étienne rolled his bullish neck across his beefy shoulders, frustrated that he still didn't know the name of the leader of *les Loups*. But he—the relentless hunter who'd been tracking them for four long years—would sure as hell find out.

****

Yvette announced her return with the recognizable pattern of knocks. She unlocked the front door and carried the block of ice into the cottage where Jules and Beau were seated at the kitchen table, shucking the oysters from her morning harvest.

Her brother rose to his feet, took the frozen slab from her straining arms, and placed it in the icebox. "How was the trek into town? Did you run into the Butcher?"

Pulse racing, limbs quivering, her eyes brimmed with sudden tears. She nodded, meeting Jules' interrogating gaze. "Yes," she stammered, her voice choking on a sob. "Jules—they've captured one of *les Loups*!"

He cursed, spinning away in frustrated rage. Fists clenched at his side, Jules stared sightlessly out the window where the pretty floral curtains fluttered on the soft summer breeze.

"They'll torture him...force him to reveal your names. And the location of the cave in the woods. Jules, you must move *les Loups*. The Butcher's men will know where to find you!" Yvette clutched his arm, begging him to listen.

Jules whipped his head toward her, his resolute expression as hard as granite. "We have code names for this very reason. If anyone is caught, they can't give us up. Only Briac, Gwilherm, Pierrick, and I know each other's real names. To everyone else, I'm just *Garou*." A wicked grin broke across his wolfish face, lupine eyes ablaze. "As for knowing our location…we'll let the Butcher's men come to us. The hunters will become the hunted. We'll capture and kill *les miliciens.* Disfigure the victims with the distinctive mark of the wolf's claw. And leave the mutilated corpses as a warning—that we savage wolves fiercely defend our beloved Breton woods."

The wolf's claw. A petrified paw with razor-sharp talons from an actual wolf. Les Loups use it to slash the faces of their victims. Branding the corpses with their identifying mark. Claiming the kill. Jules won't relocate his pack. He'll lure la Milice into a deadly trap.

Yvette rose onto tiptoes and kissed her glowering brother's bearded cheek. "I have to finish unloading the wagon." She smiled at Beau, directing his attention to the bags on the floor in the corner of the kitchen. "My neighbor, Jacques Blanchard, gave us this fleece. I'll teach you how to card and comb the wool. With your help, I'll be able to make more blankets and clothing for *les Loups.*"

She approached Jules' tense back and affectionately massaged her brother's rigid shoulders, attempting to assuage his frustrated fury at the loss of one of his pack brothers. "Even in summer, the nights are damp and cold. And the winters are brutal." As Jules shook off his anger and sat back down at the table to resume his interrupted task, Yvette took a deep breath and smiled at the two men. "I'm glad you're shucking the oysters. We'll have them with the scallops tonight. So I can stuff you with seafood before you leave." She kissed Jules' scruffy cheek, heartened by his chuckling scoff. "Be right back."

Making a couple more trips to the wagon, Yvette carried the sacks of flour, corn, and oats—along with the three loaves of bread—into the kitchen, setting them down on the counter while the men shucked the shellfish. She filled a large vat with water and set it on the stove to heat before storing the provisions in the pantry. "First, I have to remove the impurities from the wool," she explained to Beau. "I'll soak some of the fleece in hot, soapy water. We'll card and comb that so I can spin it into yarn for knitting gloves and socks. But for these," she said, referring to the two largest bags, "I'll boil the wool to shrink it. Pound it in a process known as *fulling*—to make it dense and thick. Perfect for blankets, hats, and coats. That's what *les Loups* need most."

"I'll be glad to help in any way I can." Beau flashed her a disarming grin that made her heart flutter before returning his attention to oyster shucking with Jules.

"Be back in a minute. I have a few more items to unload." Yvette returned to the wagon, fetched the bag of coal for the stove, and brought it into the kitchen. With one last trip, she brought in the remaining provisions, including the soap, candles, cooking oil, and cloth for Beau's bandages. "Want a cup of chicory?" she asked the two gruffly handsome men working at her oak table. "I'm going to have one before I return the mule and wagon to Madame Dubois."

"Sounds good." Beau's bright blue gaze glinted in the afternoon sunlight.

Jules grunted, slanting Beau a sideward glance out of the corner of his eye.

Yvette prepared three cups and set them on the table.

"I need to go." Jules wiped off his hunting knife and rose, preparing to depart.

"Not yet. *La Milice* will see you leave the cottage. You need to stay until dark. And I need you here with Beau while I return the wagon to Madame Dubois. Now, sit down and drink this." She placed a steaming cup in front of her stubborn, scowling brother, who huffed but retook his seat. Kissing his scarred, bearded cheek, she said cheerfully, despite the tremors in her limbs, "Let's enjoy another meal together tonight before you leave. We have so very few…" She hugged his shaggy head to her chest, his hacked-off black hair tickling the base of her throat. Her voice quavered under the persistent, pervasive fear of her brother's capture. "I love you, Jules. Please…*stay alive.*"

His calloused hand lovingly squeezed her arm. "I love you, too, *ma petite soeur.*" Jules kissed the hand she'd placed under his neck. "And I promise I'll do my best to stay alive. For you. For *les Loups*. And for Lola." Love-light blazed in his fierce, feral gaze.

Yvette sat down between Jules and Beau, the three of them savoring the cups of chicory in contemplative, companionable silence. When they'd finished, she collected the empty mugs, rinsed them in the sink, and kissed her brother's cheek goodbye. "I'm off to return Suzette and the wagon. Will you please add the wool to the water on the stove when it begins to boil? Turn off the heat, stir in the powdered soap, and just let it soak. I'll rinse it out when I get back."

She spoke gently but firmly to Beau. "You need to lie down and rest. Try to sleep for a while. It will help you recover more quickly." Yvette nearly swooned at his tantalizing smile as he nodded in agreement. "Be back soon."

Leaving her brother and the handsome American

soldier at the kitchen table, Yvette locked her front door. Climbed into the saddle. And drove the mule-led wagon back to the baker's house in the dense Breton woods.

Chapter 5

Carpe Diem

"The wound looks good. There's no sign of infection. You'll still need the splint for a few more weeks, but I'll leave the torn skin uncovered so it will heal more quickly. And remove the stitches next week." Yvette tenderly washed Beau's broken leg, rinsing the soapy water into the tin bucket on the kitchen floor. She reapplied the antiseptic ointment, placed soft, clean wool inside the splints, and rewrapped the fracture. "I'd like to wash your hair," she said as she removed the bandaging from his head. "I'll go pump another bucket of water from the well. And set up a chair for you near the sink. Be right back."

She went out the back door of her kitchen and descended the stone steps, the morning sun gentle upon her upturned face. The hens pecked at the grass in the backyard; larks chirped and trilled in the woods behind the cottage. *I'll pick some blueberries and make a pie to go with the rabbit stew. A few sprigs of rosemary and thyme…some carrots. There are three potatoes left, too. With a bit of lard…it will be tender and delicious. Beau will love it.*

Yvette filled the wooden bucket with water from the pump and hauled it back up the stairs into the kitchen.

She set it down on the counter beside the sink and smiled at the handsome soldier watching her with enigmatic blue eyes. "I'll have you sit here and lean back so I can pour the water over your head." She placed one of the four wooden kitchen chairs near the sink and folded a towel for Beau's neck. "All set. Come on over."

Beau rose from the table, hobbled across the kitchen, and laid his crutches against the counter. He settled onto the seat and leaned back over the sink.

She poured some of the water through his hair and lathered it up with a bar of soap, gently washing the wound with delicate fingers. As she leaned over Beau, her breasts pushed against his arm, but she didn't pull away. A sensuous shiver slivered up her spine.

"Mmm...that feels incredible." The deep rumble of Beau's baritone reverberated through her bones as she tenderly massaged his scalp. She wondered if he meant the caress of her nimble fingers or the pressure of her soft breasts against his sinewy shoulder.

Or both.

When she'd rinsed away all of the soap, he sat up so she could towel dry and comb his hair. He hummed softly with pleasure.

"I don't need to wrap your head in bandages anymore. Like the wound on your leg, this one will heal much faster if I leave it exposed to the air." Yvette delicately applied the antiseptic salve to the scab partially hidden in Beau's thick, dark hair, running her fingers through the soft, damp waves.

As she removed her hand from his head, he grabbed it, flattening it against his stubbled cheek. He closed his eyes and emitted a low, husky moan as he kissed the inside of her palm. Beau looked up at her, his alluring gaze like a limpid pool of cool, inviting water. Lust and longing glimmered in the enticing blue depths.

He wrapped an arm behind her back. Pulled her down onto his lap. And, lifting her chin with a curved finger, gently touched her lips with his own.

Soft, silky skin brushed hers as he traced the inner lining of her parted lips with the tender tip of his tongue. Angling his head for better access, he deepened the kiss, probing every recess of her opened mouth. Ardor increasing with each thrust of his bold tongue, his hardened body pressed firmly against her soft rump, sending waves of throbbing warmth to settle between her trembling thighs.

He crushed her against his broad chest, his musky scent engulfing her in flames of desire. Leaning her back in his arms, his ravenous mouth assailed her long neck as he unbuttoned the front of her cotton dress. He unfastened her bra, trailing kisses down her throat to lavish his attention on her tingling, aching breasts. When his warm lips latched firmly onto a nipple, the rhythmic tug and pull sent waves of pleasure rippling to her inner core.

His deep voice primal and raw, he groaned, "God, Yvette. I want you. Please…either straddle me in this chair. Or come with me to my bed. Let me make love to you."

Memories flashed through Yvette's mind. Passionate kisses in the hayloft of her family's barn. Her first love, Jean-Claude, his soft brown eyes like melted milk chocolate as he begged to make to love to her. But she'd refused, telling him she wanted to wait until they were married. And then…he'd been killed. In the same Nazi bombing of Paris that had claimed the lives of

Lola's parents.

June 3, 1940.

She hadn't looked at another man since Jean-Claude's death. Never felt a hint of attraction.

Until now.

Beau would leave her in a few short weeks. To rejoin his regiment and return to battle. Neither of them knew if they'd even survive this damned war. Tomorrow might never come. But they did have today. And Yvette vowed that she wouldn't make the same mistake twice.

He'd leave her, yes.

But with fond memories instead of bitter regret.

Life was ephemeral. Fragile. Fleeting. Love was a rare, precious gift. This time, she would grab the chance for happiness and seize the day.

Carpe diem.

Drowning in the depths of Beau's liquid gaze, swept into a maelstrom of desire, Yvette rose from his lap. Unbuttoned dress falling to her waist, unfastened bra tumbling unheeded to the floor, bare breasts aching for his eager lips…she helped him ease onto the crutches.

And, quivering with anticipation, led her alluring American soldier to the beckoning bed.

****

The saline scent of the nearby sea floated in on the briny breeze, fluttering the white lace curtains draped in the two large, open windows. Beau glimpsed the tall hedgerow, dense shrubs, and abundant leafy trees enshrouding the backyard in a thick, green wall of natural privacy. He laid the crutches against the wall and—balancing on his good leg, bracing himself against the sturdy bed—pulled Yvette toward him with eager, shaking hands.

Light pink nipples, stiffening in the cool morning air, topped the soft globes of her creamy white breasts. Unable to resist them, Beau lowered his ravenous lips to suckle first one, then the other, the deep moan of pleasure from Yvette's throat driving him wild.

Unbuttoning the rest of her dress with clumsy fingers, he let it fall to the floor. His eyes locked with hers as he slid her panties down over her hips.

And feasted his gaze on the glorious body of a goddess.

Full breasts filled her slender torso, her narrow waist curving onto rounded hips. And between her long, lithe legs, a tantalizing triangle of soft, dark curls.

With gentle fingers, he parted the tender pink flesh. Lowering himself into a sitting position on the edge of the bed, he drew her toward him. Spread her legs apart. And replaced his delicate, inquisitive fingers with a searching, probing tongue.

Her tangy, salty sweetness filled his senses, the stimulating scent of her arousal creating a painful ache in his loins. He laid her down upon the bed beside him and rose to stand upon his good leg. Her eyes aflame, she watched with bated breath as he removed his shirt, unzipped his pants, and released his throbbing shaft.

He knelt on the bed, hovering over her, nudging her thighs apart with powerful hands.

"Your leg…" Concern clouded her amorous gaze as she glanced at the splinted fracture laid carefully upon the bed behind him.

"Shhh," he whispered, swallowing her lips into his own. "My upper legs are *strong*."

Beau worshipped her like a deity, his reverent mouth exalting her sublime, supple skin. He caressed the length of her elegant neck and suckled her irresistible nipples, the tip of his tongue tracing and tasting the luscious lips between her lean legs.

She writhed beneath him, moaning in agonizing delight, as he penetrated her with nimble fingers and licked the little nub at the apex of her thighs. "I can't bear it...the pleasure is so intense..."

Beau lapped at her sensitive folds, increasing the urgency of his thrusts, matching the rhythm until she melted in his mouth, contracting and clenching his fingers in climax. He grinned down at her, licking his lips. "Delectable. Like the nectar of a rare flower."

Yvette purred like a contented cat, running her fingers through the ample hair across his chest. She lifted her torso up, nuzzling her nose in the dense brown curls, moaning softly as she inhaled deeply. "I love your chest hair. And your scent..."

His persistent, throbbing ache still unfulfilled, he rubbed the tip of his aroused shaft between her slippery folds, parting the enticing, moist flesh. "I must have you, Yvette. *Let me in*." With a guttural groan, he slid his hands under her rounded hips. Tilted her receptive pelvis up.

And plunged into paradise.

She wrapped her arms around his back, her legs around his waist, pulling him deeper inside. Her tight sheath clamped him like a slick vice, the lush warmth of her fiery core enveloping him in molten velvet. Unable to hold back any longer, he arrowed into her.

Erupted with volcanic force.

And filled her delicious depths with plumes of liquid flame.

After a few moments, he lay down beside her,

shifting his wounded leg. He pulled her into his arms and cradled her over his pounding heart.

She stroked the dark chest hair and nuzzled the soft curls. "I will never forget this day, Beau. Thank you for making my first time so memorable."

He held her, savoring the sated glow in his loins and the solace in his soul. "I'll always remember today, too." Beau kissed her wild mane of tousled black curls. "I wish I could remember the past. I don't even know my own damned name."

She twirled his chest hair into little peaks, then brushed them out with a flattened palm. "Your memory will return. Maybe slowly…little by little." Her piercing, pale eyes peered deeply into his as she rose up onto an elbow to gaze down at him. "Or perhaps…something will trigger your memory. And everything will come flooding back all at once."

He pushed a curling tendril from her pensive, beautiful face. "I have had a few flashbacks. Vague memories." Long black locks cascaded over his arm as he caressed her bare shoulder. "I remember being a child…climbing to the top of a tall pine tree in a dense forest. Deep snow everywhere. So…I must have lived in a northern climate." He stroked the soft skin on her cheek, trying to retrace the elusive past. "I used to play baseball in an open, grassy field. With an older boy. I think he's my brother."

Her eyes flashed with fire as she settled onto her stomach, supporting herself with bent elbows. "That's wonderful! Your memory *is* starting to return."

"I also have visions of a woman. Soft brown hair streaked with grey. Gentle hands, a loving smile. She must be my mother." He held Yvette's rapt gaze, her silvery eyes sparkling like mirrors in the morning light. "But...I hear her piercing, keening wail of grief. Something terrible happened. I just can't remember what. And when I see her face, a heavy sadness grips my heart in a tight, smothering vice. I wish I knew why."

Yvette slid her arms underneath his back, wrapping him in a comforting embrace, as she rested her head upon his chest. "You'll remember...once you've fully healed. It's a good sign that some of your memories are returning." She kissed the dark hair on his chest, inhaling his scent deep into her lungs. "But in the meantime...you and I will make new ones. Memories to last us both a lifetime."

She raised herself up to straddle him with her thighs, rubbing the moist, tender flesh between her legs against his thickening arousal. Leaning over him, black curls cascading around his shoulders, she engulfed his lips with her own. Reaching behind her hips, she grasped his erect shaft.

And guided him into warm, welcoming bliss.

Later, as they lay together, limbs carefully entwined, she murmured, "I need to prepare dinner." She rose from the bed, smoothed her hair, and bent down to kiss him. "And you need sleep, to recover from your injuries. So...while I simmer a savory rabbit stew and make an incredible blueberry pie...you take a nap. And join me in the kitchen when you wake up." She tucked the covers around his neck as he snuggled into the pillow, humming with pleasure. "*Dors, mon chou.* Sleep well."

Beau smiled as he closed his heavy eyelids. For the very first time, Yvette had addressed him in French with the familiar form reserved for friends.

Family.

And lovers.

His body sated and his heart full, Beau drifted off to peaceful, restorative sleep.

****

A couple of hours later, Beau emerged from the bedroom and maneuvered on his crutches into the kitchen. "Something smells delicious." Blue eyes sparkling in the afternoon sun, he watched her remove two pies from the oven and set them on cooling racks upon the counter.

"Blueberry pie for us, and a *tarte aux mirabelles* for Jacques and Lola Blanchard." Yvette smiled as Beau approached and hovered over the simmering pot.

"Mmm," he murmured, inhaling the sumptuous aromas of garlic, rosemary, and thyme. "You're an amazing cook." A corner of his sensuous mouth curled up into an adorable, boyish grin. "I'm starved. When do we eat?"

She chuckled, realizing how long it had been since she'd laughed. "Now." Yvette leaned over and kissed him, her happy heart full.

"The flavor is incredible, and the meat is so tender…" Beau scooped another heaping forkful into his mouth, sopping up rich gravy with the hearty, grainy bread. He raised his glass of red wine in tribute to Yvette. "My compliments to the chef."

Enormously pleased with his genuine enjoyment of her cuisine and the flattering praise, Yvette sipped her wine and beamed. "Thank you. I'm glad you like it."

He appreciated the blueberry pie as much as the meal, finishing off two large pieces with flourish. "You're going to the Blanchard's tomorrow?" he asked, eyeing the *tarte aux mirabelles* on the counter.

"Mm hm. I'm going to harvest seafood at dawn. The tide will be low, perfect for gathering scallops and digging clams. I'll bring the pie in the wagon with me and give it to them when I deliver the shellfish." Yvette finished her wine, arose from the table, and took their empty dishes to the sink.

She shot a sidelong glance at him, unease gripping her heart. "I think it's best if you hide in the cellar while I'm gone." She washed and rinsed a plate, setting it in the dishrack to dry. "Ever since the Butcher's men caught one of *les Loups,* they're scouring the forest, searching for the rest of the pack. And they're hunting for you—the American soldier whose plane was shot down. Whose parachute was blown into our Breton woods." She walked over to him and stroked his soft brown hair. His stared up at her, his expression as turbulent as the tumultuous sea. "When I'm here, I can stall anyone who comes to the door. But if you're alone...with your crutches...you won't have enough time to hide." She lifted his chin and kissed his smooth, strained lips. "I'd feel much safer it if you went down there before I leave."

The stark reality dimmed his bright, shrewd gaze. He nodded in reluctant acquiescence. "All right. I'll agree to your request." Impish, seductive delight glimmered in his dark blue gaze. "But I want you to do something for me, too."

"And what would that be?" she asked coyly, caressing his bearded cheek. Her heart accelerated at the amorous gleam in his sultry eyes.

"Move into my bedroom. Sleep with me. For whatever length of time we have left. I want to savor every moment with you. And treasure the memories forever." He cradled her hand in his, brushing soft lips against her trembling fingers.

"With pleasure." She wrapped her hands behind his head as he raised his eager mouth to hers. A shiver of delight rippled up her spine at the thought of sleeping with him every night. *We'll make love as often as possible. And make the most of our time together.*

As his hungry lips tugged on hers, he whispered huskily into her opened mouth. "Let's go make some memorable moments right now."

****

A while later, Yvette returned to the kitchen with Beau, her loins aglow, her heart content. She poured them each a cup of chicory as Beau settled into a chair at the oak table. "We still have a couple hours left before dark. I need to card and comb the remainder of this wool." She pointed to the last of the three bags Jacques Blanchard had given her. "And gather herbs from my garden to make more salve for your wounds."

Beau jutted his chin to the bag on the floor and patted the oak table. "I'll take care of the wool right here while you go collect what you need outside." His eager expression lit up his bruised, bristled face.

"That would be fabulous. If you card and comb this for me, I'll go gather the herbs and harvest a few vegetables from the garden for supper." She set him up with the tools and the bag of wool, bending down to kiss his stubbled cheek. "If you can help me process the wool over the next few weeks as you recover, I'll be able to make even more blankets and warm clothing for *les Loups* this winter. That would be incredible, and I'd be most grateful." She hugged his healing head against her chest, smoothed his tousled hair, and went outside to collect the herbs. A short while later, she returned to the kitchen with an ample, bountiful harvest.

While Beau worked the wool at the table, Yvette ground the herbs and prepared the salve, which she stored with her medicinal supplies. She whipped up an *omelette aux épinards* with fresh spinach from the garden for each of them, topping her culinary creations with mushrooms and grated *brebis* cheese from Jacques Blanchard's sheep.

When Beau finished combing the wool, she put it aside, ready to spin the following day. She wiped off the table, set it for supper, and the two of them enjoyed the simple, wholesome meal.

Yvette went back outside to house the chickens in the coop for the night. After securing the windows and doors of the cottage, she followed Beau into his bedroom, where they made love in the moonlight shining through the sheltered forest.

And—cocooned in the sinewy arms of her handsome American soldier—she slept soundly for the first time in four years.

Chapter 6

Russian Wolfhounds

Early the following morning, Yvette prepared boiled oats, honey, and strawberries with the last of the milk from Jacques Blanchard's sheep. She and Beau finished the humble but nutritious breakfast at the kitchen table in the predawn hours before she headed to the cove in the Cancale Bay to harvest shellfish.

"It's dangerous for you to venture alone through the dark woods. Do you at least have a weapon?" Beau scowled, his brows furrowed in apprehension. He watched her clear away the dishes, quickly wash the two bowls and spoons, and set them in the drainer to dry. She rinsed out the empty bottle of milk, which she would return to Jacques Blanchard, along with the two clean ones now sitting on the kitchen counter.

"I do indeed," she replied, sheathing a jagged hunting knife into a leather pouch belted at her waist. "And I have a dagger, strapped to my ankle." Yvette removed her foot from a rubber boot, pulling her pant leg up to reveal the concealed weapon. She held his wary gaze, concern clouding his countenance, as she slipped her foot inside, tucking the garment back in place. "And I know how to use them. I grew up with three brothers who taught me how to fight." She approached the chair where he sat and softly stroked his stubbled cheek. "I'll be careful. I always go to a secluded inlet, far from watchful, suspicious eyes."

Beau kissed the inside of her palm. His rugged, calloused hand was shaking. *He's worried about me. And frustrated that there's nothing he can do to protect me.*

"Come, I'll help you hide in the cellar under the bed. I need to go now, while it's still dark. When the tide is low." She helped him with the crutches and led him into the bedroom. Pushing away the bed, she crouched down and pressed on the distinctive knot in the pinewood floor.

When the panel popped up, she pulled it to one side, revealing the dark earthen floor underneath, deep within the foundation of the cottage. "Hand me your crutches. I'll pass them to you once you're safely on the ground."

Beau complied. He sat at the edge of the hole in the floor and lowered himself carefully down to the dirt. Balancing on his good leg, he braced against the column which supported the cottage. "OK, pass me the crutches."

Yvette lowered the carved wooden sticks with soft wool padding at the shoulders. When Beau leaned them against the structural wall of the foundation, Yvette handed him the chamber pot. "You might need this."

"I hate that you have to empty this for me. It's humiliating." He reluctantly accepted the large bowl and placed it on the ground near the crutches.

"Well, you certainly can't use the outhouse. Someone might see you. This is our only option. At least I can use the urine for fulling the wool." She grinned down at his incredulous expression.

"You use my urine to process the wool?" Beau's mouth was agape in shock.

71

"Absolutely. Fulling has been done that way ever since the Middle Ages. The ammonia in the urine breaks down the bonds in the fleece, making the wool dense and compact. Perfect for winter coats and warm blankets." She laughed at his disgusted grimace.

"I must admit, you're resourceful." He shook his head with a smirk, then glanced up at her. Regret and resignation warred on his worried brow. "Be careful. I can't bear to think of you getting hurt. Or captured." Anguish blazed in his bitter eyes. "I wish I could go with you. To defend you." His mouth tightened grimly at the impossibility of that desire. "Hurry back, so I know you're safe."

"I will. And remember—if you hear anything, hide behind the column. And wait for the signature knock to know I've returned." She lowered his canteen through the opening in the floor. "Here's some fresh water. I filled it this morning." Yvette stood and gazed down at him, uneasy at the thought of leaving him alone. "I'll be gone for a few hours. But I'll be back as quickly as I can. See you soon. *À bientôt.*" Her heart heavy, filled with dread at the thought of what would happen to him if she didn't return, Yvette replaced the wooden panel in the floor and slid the bed back over to cover it. Scanning the room to be sure none of Beau's clothing or personal items remained in sight, she went into the kitchen. Fetched the empty milk bottles to return to Jacques. Locked the front door behind her. And, retrieving her hand-pulled wagon from the shed beside the cottage, ventured off into the dark woods toward the sheltered sea cove on the craggy coast.

****

Marie-Claire Dubois came out of her cottage, drying

her hands on a towel, her dour expression a mask of irritation. "Where were you this morning? Marcel waited as long as he could to hitch the wagon for you. But he had to leave—to open the bakery in town and start up the ovens. Everyone in the village needs bread. He couldn't wait any longer." She stormed down the steps, clearly disgruntled, to examine the contents of Yvette's small wagon. "When you never showed up to borrow the mule, I went to your cottage to see if you were ill. I knocked on the back door and peered into the kitchen." Marie-Claire's beady eyes were angry and suspicious. "There were several bags of fleece, some combed wool, and a spinning wheel. What are you making with all that wool? And where are you getting the supply?"

Yvette's pulse raced as her mouth went dry. *I have to think fast. She'll turn me in to the Butcher. And I don't want to endanger Jacques and Lola.* "I'm...making blankets for the German army," she lied, trying to calm her quavering voice. "I plan to bring them into town with me the next time I go for supplies." She forced a stilted smile, summoning courage that she did not feel. "Would it be possible for me to borrow Suzette and the wagon...when the time comes to transport them into the village?" The thought of sacrificing some of the blankets so desperately needed by *les Loups* to aid the Nazis turned Yvette's stomach, but it was the only plausible way to hide the truth. *I'll have to donate four blankets to la Milice. But I'll keep six for les Loups. And hope Jacques has enough wool to make four more.*

"Why didn't you come to borrow the mule this morning? Marcel waited nearly an hour for you." Marie-Claire's shrill voice was the cackle of a shrew. Dark, dubious eyes scrutinized Yvette's flustered face.

"I am so sorry to have inconvenienced your husband. I decided not to borrow Suzette because I didn't want to abuse your generosity. I know you must feed her extra hay when she works for me." Yvette gestured to her small wagon. "I can pull this myself and spare you the additional expense. Please accept my apology." *The real reason I didn't want to borrow the mule is because I don't want to be all the more indebted to you. I don't even like bartering with you at all. But I need the bread, flour, and oats for Beau. And the corn for my hens.*

"Well, next time there's a change in plans, at least have the decency to let us know in advance." Madame Dubois harrumphed with disdain, directing her greedy attention to the succulent shellfish in the back of the wooden wagon. "What have you brought me today?"

"Some delectable scallops and clams. The tide was low, so I was able to harvest them this time." Yvette handed a bucket of each type of crustacean to the irritated, impatient baker's wife.

"Thank you. Stay here. I'll be right back." Marie-Claire carried the seafood into her cottage and returned the empty buckets to Yvette. She went back into the cottage and came out with two parcels and two loaves of bread. "Here are the items Marcel left for you." She handed Yvette a cotton sack of flour, a burlap bag of corn, and two loaves of *pain de campagne*.

Yvette noted the absence of the sack of oats that the baker had promised. "Excuse me, Madame, but there is supposed to be a sack of oats as well. Could you have perhaps forgotten it?" She hoped her polite tone would placate the plump, glowering woman whose stringy grey hair was plastered to her frowning forehead.

You left that bag in the kitchen on purpose. To

penalize me for making Marcel wait. You're a grumpy, selfish hag.

"Let me check." Madame Dubois huffed in exasperation and stomped up the stairs. She returned a few moments later with a sack of oats, which she thrust at Yvette. "Here. I must have missed it somehow."

Of course, you did. A simple, honest mistake. Yvette scoffed silently and audibly thanked Madame Dubois. "Would you please convey my apologies to your husband for today's inconvenience?" She secured the empty wooden buckets into the back of the wagon and looked up at the cynical crone. "I'll be back this Saturday with more seafood. Until then, I bid you good day. *Au revoir, Madame.*" Yvette checked the contents in her wooden cart and prepared to depart.

"You haven't been into town this week, so you haven't heard the news, have you?" Madame Dubois was positively salivating at the salacious gossip she was obviously eager to share.

A ripple of dread shivered up Yvette's spine. "No…what news?"

"You remember how *la Milice* apprehended one of *les Loups*? Well, now that Étienne Boucher knows where the Resistance rebels are hiding in the woods, he plans to travel to the village of Cancale. There's a high-ranking German officer and his SS men lodging in a seized farmhouse there. On a cliff overlooking the sea. The perfect location to observe enemy ships. A lookout point and military garrison."

Yvette's stomach dropped. It couldn't be. The same Nazis who confiscated her family farm. The same SS officer who ordered his men to gun down her father and brothers. Yvette's hands shook, and her knees nearly buckled at the stark realization. A farmhouse on a cliff. Overlooking the sea. In the coastal village of Cancale.

Her former family home.

"Étienne Boucher plans to meet with the SS Officer. To requisition three dozen Russian Wolfhounds." Marie-Claire's dark gaze glinted with malicious glee. "To hunt *les Loups*."

Yvette swallowed, her throat constricting in fear. Her legs shook inside her khaki trousers. "Russian Wolfhounds. You mean…*dogs*?"

Madame Dubois cackled and sneered. "No, foolish girl. Not dogs. Former Soviet prisoners. Men who were beaten and tortured. Starved in Russian gulags." She snickered with garish delight. "The Nazis offered them hefty rations. Rifles. Proper treatment. And—most important of all—their freedom. In exchange for working with the German army." Gloating over the tantalizing tidbit, the baker's wife crooned, "They'll round up those damned Resistance rebels. Hunt them down like rabid dogs. And destroy every last one of the filthy, traitorous *Loups.*"

Jules and les Loups are in grave danger. The Butcher knows where to hunt. And—with three dozen Russian Wolfhounds—he'll track them. Capture them. And kill them all. I have to warn him right away.

"Étienne Boucher is going to Cancale this Friday, to meet with the Nazi officer and requisition the Wolfhounds. He'll rid these woods of those pesky wolves once and for all." Madame Dubois crossed her arms over her plump bosom, harrumphing in stern satisfaction and acerbic approval.

"I'm certain he will." Smiling courteously to conceal her distress, Yvette turned away from the baker's wife and grasped the handle of her wagon, steadying her wobbly legs. "*Au revoir, Madame. Bonne journée.*"

"Good day to you as well, Yvette. See you Saturday." With a hungry, hawklike stare, Marie-Claire Dubois watched Yvette continue along the beaten path at the edge of the forest.

And into the dense Breton woods.

****

"Russian Wolfhounds?" Jacques Blanchard scowled, his confounded expression grim.

Yvette accepted the cup of chicory from Lola, who pulled up an oak chair and joined her grandfather and their welcome guest at the kitchen table in the cozy wood cabin. "Yes. Marie-Claire Dubois told me that the Butcher is going to Cancale later this week to meet with the SS officer and requisition three dozen of them. To hunt *les Loups*." Tears blurred her vision as she beheld Jacques' wrinkled, worried face. "I must warn Jules."

The shrewd old farmer arose from the table and walked across the kitchen to gaze out the window at his grazing sheep. Contemplative, he turned toward Yvette, his brow furrowed in concentration. "I suspect Marie-Claire Dubois is one of the Butcher's informants. She might have leaked that information to you deliberately. So that you would lure Jules into a trap."

Yvette couldn't breathe. "But I must warn him somehow." She averted her gaze from Lola's impassioned, distraught expression, focusing instead on the bitter brew inside her ceramic cup.

"Leave a note under the boulder at the edge of the cave." Jacques came back to the table and took hold of Yvette's trembling hand. "Briac will see you leave it there. And retrieve it when he can. He'll take the message to Jules."

Briac, whose code name was *Singe*—Monkey—was the lookout for *les Loups*. Always perched high in a tall pine tree, he scanned the forest for messengers. Or spies. And signaled the bird call to alert or warn the pack.

"I'll do that. But I must leave now. Thank you for the cup of chicory. And the hospitality." Yvette hugged Lola, whose soft brown curls tickled her cheek. "I'll be back Saturday with more shellfish."

Lola squeezed her hands affectionately, eyeing the wild plum tart on the kitchen counter. "Thank you so much for the *tarte aux mirabelles*. *Papi* and I will savor every delicious bite." She smiled at her doting grandfather, whose kind visage crinkled with gratitude. "Be careful," she warned Yvette, imploring her with large, expressive eyes. "Make certain you're not followed. The Butcher's spies are everywhere." Lola kissed her two cheeks with *la bise* of farewell. "Until Saturday. *À bientôt*. See you soon."

Jacques kissed Yvette goodbye as well, the bristles of his white beard scratching her skin. "I loaded up two more bags of wool. Another wheel of *brebis* cheese. And three bottles of sheep's milk. Thank you for the seafood. And the *tarte aux mirabelles*." His wary eyes were full or warning. "Be extra cautious, Yvette. Marie-Claire Dubois can't be trusted."

"I will. And thank you both. For everything. See you Saturday." Yvette smiled and left the warm kitchen, glad they were so appreciative of her homemade pie.

Jacques and Lola followed her to the door of their wooden cabin, waving as she continued west along the path at the edge of the woods, heading back to her cottage.

And the handsome American soldier hiding in the cellar.

****

Beau eased himself into the chair at the kitchen table as Yvette stored the cheese, milk, and seafood in the icebox. "When you were gone, I heard someone knocking at the back door. And a woman's voice, calling through the bedroom window right above me." He accepted the cup of chicory with a grateful nod. "I hid behind the column, like you said. And left my backpack there. Might as well leave it hidden until I need it."

"Marie-Claire Dubois—she's the baker's wife I barter with for flour, oats, bread, and corn. I suspect she's one of the Butcher's informants. She's nosy, suspicious…greedy. And always spreading gossip." Yvette placed a platter of oysters in front of Beau, who began shucking them for dinner. "Madame Dubois told me that Étienne Boucher—the Butcher—is traveling to the village of Cancale later this week. He's meeting with a Nazi officer there, requesting a regiment of three dozen former Soviet prisoners. So that they can help him scour the woods and hunt *les Loups.*"

Yvette approached Beau, her limbs shaking. "The Gestapo officer and his regiment are lodging in a seized farmhouse. On the edge of a craggy cliff. In the coastal village of Cancale." Painful images of the past crashed against her like ocean waves pummeling the rocky point. "Where my family had a farmhouse. On the edge of a cliff. Overlooking the sea."

Tears blurred her vision as she whispered, her barely audible voice quavering with horror. "The Butcher is meeting with same Nazi who gunned down my father and brothers."

Her knees buckled, and Beau caught her, pulling her onto his lap and enveloping her in strong, sheltering arms. He kissed her hair, her face, and her neck.

She cried on his chest as he stroked her wild mane of long black curls.

He lifted her chin, lowered his lips to hers.

And swallowed her sorrow.

His eager mouth devoured hers, his hands caressing her skin, wiping the tears from her stained cheeks. He stroked her neck, her shoulders, her breasts. Unbuttoning and removing her shirt, he unfastened and peeled off her bra. Trailing kisses down her throat, he assailed her aching nipples with warm lips and skilled tongue.

Yvette's sobs of sorrow became whimpers of want as he rubbed his hardened length against her rump. She rose to her feet, handed him the crutches. And led him to the beckoning bed.

She threw off the rest of her clothes and stood naked before him, quivering with desire. Yvette unbuttoned and removed Beau's shirt, running her fingers through the dark hair on his chest, moaning as his scent enflamed her senses.

He unzipped his fly, releasing his erect shaft.

Yvette trembled as he pushed his jeans down his long, lean legs.

Beau sat on the edge of the bed and took off his pants. Longing and lust blazed in his impassioned gaze as he pulled her toward him. He suckled her breasts until she swooned. Laid her on the bed. Positioned himself between her shaking thighs.

And impaled her with a guttural groan.

Yvette clutched his muscled back, wrapped her legs

around his thrusting hips. And melted around his erupting staff.

A while later, he reclined beside her, cradling her head on his damp chest. He kissed her tousled hair. "You are bewitching. Breathtaking. Beautiful. I can't get enough of you."

She burrowed her nose into the dark hair on his chest and inhaled his scent deep into her lungs. "Thank you for washing away the horror of the past. By immersing me in the pleasure of the present." She kissed his full, soft lips, reveling in the sensual delight. "You must be hungry. Let's go back to the kitchen. We can eat the oysters, and I'll sauté the scallops with fresh herbs from the garden. There's a loaf of nutty *pain de campagne*, and we can have strawberries and wild plums for dessert. Sound good?"

A hearty grin spread across his handsome, stubbled face. "Sounds incredible. I'm starved."

****

Yvette's heart was full as she watched Beau savor every sumptuous bite of the seafood feast she'd prepared. The oysters were succulent, the scallops sweet, and the fresh fruit was bursting with ripe, rich flavor. She sipped her glass of mint water, content with his comforting presence. And obvious enjoyment of their midday meal.

At least he'll have a full stomach when he goes back down into the cellar to hide. Because I need to deliver the warning message to Jules. And tell les Loups about the Russian Wolfhounds.

When Beau finished eating, he complimented her culinary talents. "That was *delicious*." He took hold of her hand and raised it to his lips, dark blue eyes dancing with delight. "You are an amazing chef, Yvette Fleury."

She chuckled, thoroughly pleased with the praise. Her voice took on a suddenly somber tone. "Although I hate to ask, I need you to go back down into the cellar. So I can go to the cave in the woods and deliver a message to Jules. I'll be gone a couple of hours. I'm sorry, but I must go right away." She squeezed Beau's calloused hand. "I'm going to ask him to come here tonight. So I can tell him about the Russian Wolfhounds." A shudder of dread rippled up her spine as she held Beau's perceptive gaze. "And inform him that the Butcher is going to Cancale. To meet the Nazi officer who shot him. And killed our father and two brothers." Her stomach clenched at the implications of the fateful encounter. "I hope the Butcher's meeting is brief. And that he doesn't inquire about the family who used to live in the farmhouse."

Because if he does, he'll discover the identity of Garou. The leader of les Loups.

The elusive alpha wolf he's been hunting for years.

My beloved brother.

Jules Fleury.

Chapter 7

Predatory Instincts

Étienne Boucher drove up the long, winding dirt road toward the three-story white farmhouse with steeply peaked, grey slate gable roof in the quaint, coastal village of Cancale. Perched on a peninsula, upon a high cliff overlooking the sea, the spacious residence with mullioned windows which flanked the front door and graced its upper levels offered a spectacular view of the Mont-Saint-Michel Bay. Along opposite edges of the property on either side of the main residence, rows of military barracks housing a multitude of German soldiers lined the fields where emaciated slaves tended crops destined to feed the garrison of Nazis while they themselves starved from malnutrition. In the distance, beyond the stables housing horses and mules, a herd of sheep grazed among the grass, weeds, and abundant wildflowers in full, glorious bloom. Recently shorn for their fleece, many of the older animals who could no longer produce sufficient wool would soon be slaughtered to feed the voracious army which commandeered the strategic lookout post on the peninsular coastal point.

Inside the dependable, dark green *Citroën,* Didier—his most trusted member of *la Milice*—accompanied

Étienne to meet the high-ranking Nazi Officer, *Obersturmführer* Heinrich Balsch. Captain in the Wehrmacht army. And Senior Storm Leader in the armed branch of Hitler's Secret Service, the *Waffen-SS*.

Adrenaline surged as Étienne parked the car in front of the solid oak entrance. He was about to meet the SS Officer who could grant his request for three dozen former Soviet prisoners, transformed into formidable Nazi soldiers.

Relentless Russian Wolfhounds.

With his predatory instincts augmented by impressive Soviet manpower, Étienne would finally track down the French Resistance rebels lurking in the dense Breton woods. The *maquis* mongrels who'd eluded him for four long years. The alpha wolf *Garou* and his mangy lupine pack.

Les Loups.

Étienne saluted the German soldier who greeted him and his companion at the front door of the commandeered farmhouse. "*Heil Hitler!* We have an appointment with the *Obersturmführer*. He is expecting us."

"*Suivez-moi.* Follow me." The punctilious military escort led Étienne and Didier from the entry foyer down a narrow hall to an expansive white room which served as a reception area and office. Through the large, open windows on either side of an oval mahogany table, Étienne observed the turbulent ocean far below the craggy cliff. The crisp, saline scent of the sea wafted in on the briny breeze.

As they entered the room, an impeccably dressed Nazi Officer in a greyish green uniform with the distinctive SS insignia upon his collar arose from the table to welcome his expected guests while the escort introduced the two Frenchmen.

Tall and hefty, with dark blond hair, flat nose and square jawline outlining his stern, severe expression, *Obersturmführer* Heinrich Balsch greeted them with the hard, wary eyes of a seasoned Wehrmacht commander. "*Bonjour, Messieurs,*" the Senior Storm Leader greeted the two members of *la Milice* in badly accented French heavily laced with German. "It is a pleasure to meet you. *Asseyez-vous, je vous en prie.* Please, be seated." He gestured for coffee to be served as Étienne and Didier settled at the table into the blue velvet tufted mahogany chairs.

A servant—undoubtedly a forced laborer—retrieved an exquisite sterling silver coffee service from an ornately carved, marble-topped wooden sideboard. He placed the elegant platter with coffee pot and matching creamer and sugar bowl in the center of the table upon an ivory lace table runner. As the obedient *domestique* poured three cups from the elegant silver container, the rich aroma of the rare beverage reserved for the Reich and the privileged few filled the salty Breton air.

Étienne and his colleague gratefully accepted the porcelain cups of steaming brew and joined the SS Officer in adding cream and sugar, savoring the robust flavor of the exceedingly scarce libation.

Heinrich Balsch swallowed a gulp of coffee and methodically placed the gold-rimmed, white china cup upon its saucer. "I received your communiqué requesting an audience. Based upon your impeccable service as Section Leader of *la Milice* in the nearby village of *le Vivier-Sur-Mer,* I was most amenable to meet with you personally and hear your entreaty." The Nazi officer's polite, polished smile revealed perfect white teeth. "Please tell me, Section Leader Boucher. How may I assist you in performing your duty to the Third Reich?"

Étienne slanted a glance at Didier, then met the assessing, scrutinizing glare of the formidable SS Officer. "*Herr Obersturmführer,* I would like to requisition three dozen soldiers from the XV Cossack Cavalry Corps—the former Soviet prisoners who have agreed to serve the Nazi regime." He squared his brawny shoulders and inhaled deeply, summoning the courage to voice his request. "There is an elusive, malignant band of French Resistance rebels hiding in the dense woods near *le Vivier-Sur-Mer.* They call themselves *les Loups*—after the famed wolves of ancient Breton lore. I have been hunting them, with limited success, for four long years. However, with additional manpower from Russian Cossack soldiers, I will finally be able to round them up once and for all. And eliminate the risk of sabotage that *les Loups* pose to the Garman Wehrmacht army."

SS Officer Balsch leaned back in his chair and stretched his long, muscular legs. The gleaming black leather of his knee-high boots glistened in the morning light. "I will grant your request, Section Leader Boucher. However, I can only spare one dozen of the Soviet soldiers." Rage blazed in his stormy blue gaze, turbulent as the thunderous surf below the craggy cliff. "The Allied Forces have overtaken Normandy and seized most of the Cotentin Peninsula. They are expected to recover the deep-sea port of Cherbourg, vital for their naval forces to reinforce the invading infantry." He leaned forward in his chair to take a large swallow of coffee.

With a gloating grin, he snickered. "The German army, of course, will demolish Cherbourg, rendering it useless to the enemy. But, in the meantime…I have been ordered to gather reinforcements to fortify the nearby port of Saint-Malo, identified by the *Führer* himself as a Tower of his defensive Atlantic Wall."

Grinding his teeth as he glared at the distant white-capped waves, Heinrich Balsch directed his attention back to the two Frenchmen seated at the table. "In addition to tanks and artillery, thousands of military troops are being transported here by train. The Russian soldiers will be among them, arriving at scheduled intervals over the next two to three weeks. So, Section Leader Boucher, I will allocate one dozen Cossacks to assist you in your mission to eliminate *les Loups*." The *Obersturmführer* scrutinized Étienne with an impassive, steely stare. "And—when summoned—you and *la Milice* will join my regiment for the anticipated battle. For you see, once the Allies retake the port of Cherbourg, the Fortress of Saint-Malo must be defended at all costs."

The scowling German officer steepled his fingers in pensive concentration. "Nazi intelligence reports indicate that the Allies will soon be moving westward into Brittany, focused on acquiring key ports of entry for their naval forces. Battleships. Destroyers. Submarines. We cannot allow that to happen. You will assist me in defending the vital port of Saint-Malo, Section Leader Boucher. *To the death*."

A ripple of dread shivered down Étienne's spine, quickly dissipated by the thrill of acquiring a dozen Russian Wolfhounds to track down *les Loups*. "Thank you, *Herr Obersturmführer*." Étienne ducked his chin in a respectful bow. Awash in relief that his requisition had been granted, he admired the remarkable panoramic view as he gazed out the two large windows on opposite sides of the room. "It's no wonder you wished to obtain this farmhouse. This is the perfect spot for an observation point."

"Indeed, it is. We are uniquely positioned here to inform the *Carlingue*—Gestapo headquarters in Paris—of any Allied warships approaching the coast. When I first spotted this farmhouse perched high upon a peninsular cliff, I knew immediately that it would be the ideal location for a lookout post. With hundreds of forced laborers providing the manpower, I ordered the construction of military barracks on these premises, sufficient to house my entire regiment of five hundred men. We installed pillboxes—concrete guardhouses with heavy artillery to defend this peninsula—at strategic points along the shore. As *Obersturmführer* in the SS, and *Hauptmann* in the Wehrmacht Germany army, it is my honor and privilege to defend Hitler's Atlantic Wall."

Heinrich Balsch shook his head and scoffed, as if recalling an amusing anecdote. "The obstinate farmer who owned this land vainly tried to defend it with his three adult sons. As if they could resist the inexorable, oppressive power of the Third Reich." He chuckled darkly, a garish grin spreading across his ruthless, merciless face. "We lined them up and gunned them down. But…strangely, when I later ordered my men to dispose of the bodies—once we'd finished unloading our supplies and getting settled into the farmhouse—there were only three corpses. Not four. One of the sons had inexplicably survived. And escaped into the woods. My men searched for weeks but found no trace of him. He must have been picked up by the *maquis.* The Resistance rebels hiding in the forest. Perhaps the very group you have been hunting, Section Leader Boucher. The Wolves of the Breton Woods. *Les Loups.*"

With a sizzling jolt, every nerve in Étienne's body sparked to life as his predatory instincts kicked in.

A new trail to track and trap the alpha wolf.

Garou.

"*Herr Obersturmführer,*" Étienne began, his tone reverent and deferential, "the German army is notorious for keeping meticulous records." He leaned forward in his chair, wiping damp palms along the pants of his blue uniform as adrenaline surged in his bulging veins. "I wish to request the names of the farmer and his three sons who used to live in this farmhouse. I am especially interested in discovering the identity of the one who escaped. If he is indeed the leader of *les Loups*, as I suspect, then learning his true name will enable me to entrap him. And—once the alpha wolf is eliminated—the rest of the pack will fall."

The *Obersturmführer* pursed his thin lips and nodded, his brows furrowed in contemplation. "I will requisition Gestapo headquarters in Paris. However, with the Allied advancements in Normandy and the urgency of diverting weapons and manpower to confront that assault, the *Carlingue* offices are both overworked and understaffed. It will likely take three to four weeks to obtain that information. In the meantime, the Cassock soldiers will soon begin arriving by train." The Nazi officer consulted his calendar among the neatly stacked pile of papers on the table at his right. "Return here on the twentieth of July. I shall authorize a truck and driver to transport the Russian soldiers, following you to your headquarters in *le Vivier-Sur-Mer*. Until then, Section Leader Boucher, I bid you good day." Heinrich Balsch rose to his full, impressive height and shook Étienne's hand. "Thank you again for your impeccable service to the Third Reich. *Heil Hitler*!"

Étienne raised his right arm in the mandatory *Sieg Heil* salute as he said goodbye to the ominous *Obersturmführer. "Heil Hitler!"*

With Didier at his side, he followed the German escort back down the hall, through the front door, repeating the salute to the Nazi soldiers stationed at the farmhouse garrison. Climbing into the dark green *Citroën*, Étienne Boucher drove from the lookout point on the craggy cliff of Cancale.

Back to the Breton woods.

And the seaside village of *le Vivier-Sur-Mer.*

****

Marie-Claire Dubois was one of his most valued and trusted informants. As wife of the village baker, she knew all the local gossip and was more than eager to share defamatory news in exchange for a chocolate bar, a bag of coffee, or an occasional bottle of champagne. Although her putrid breath and pungent body odor poisoned the air he breathed, Étienne was nevertheless glad to see the snitch when Bruno—one of his dependable *miliciens*—escorted her into the room above the supply store that he had converted into an office.

Rising from his cluttered desk, he greeted her with a firm handshake and a patient, patronizing smile. "*Bonjour, Madame Dubois*. A pleasure to see you again." With a jut of his chin, he directed Bruno to leave, closing the door behind him for privacy.

This valuable information was intended solely for

his ears as Section Leader of *la Milice* in *le Vivier-Sur-Mer*.

"Good day, *Monsieur Boucher,*" the doddering biddy stammered, smoothing her frumpy, rumpled dress. "I have overheard something highly suspicious. And, as a responsible French citizen performing my duty to the German army, I am relaying that information to you as required by law." Nervous and jumpy as a weasel, the greasy hag's beady brown eyes glinted with malicious glee.

Étienne's pulse quickened. Highly suspicious rumors were the source of his power over the weak. And—under Sylvain's brutal hands and torturous devices—compromised villagers were compelled to confess. "Excellent, Madame Dubois. You are to be commended for your diligence. Now, what information do you have for me today?"

Fearful and suspicious, she glanced around the room. Ascertaining that the two of them were indeed alone, Marie-Claire divulged the urgent message she was obviously anxious to convey. "The other day, as a kind neighbor, I paid a friendly visit to Yvette Fleury."

Étienne's stomach lurched at the mention of Yvette's name. Perhaps this information would be useful indeed. He longed to ensnare Yvette Fleury. And force her to submit to his iron will.

His body thickened, becoming ramrod hard at the lascivious thought.

Madame Dubois wrung her rough, wrinkled hands in agitation. "When she didn't come to the door, I was concerned she might be ill."

Of course you were. Lying bitch. You were snooping for a tantalizing tidbit to offer me. In exchange for a fucking chocolate bar. He waited patiently for the skittish rat to continue, despite the ravenous, raging roar in his lusty loins.

"I went into her backyard and peered through the kitchen window. And there—on the floor—were bags of raw fleece, processed wool, carding combs...and a spinning wheel." The wrinkled skin around her lips puckered in a sinister sneer. "Yvette Fleury is making blankets, scarves, and gloves. I saw them with my own eyes. And yet—when I questioned her about it the next time I saw her—she told me that she is helping a neighbor make winter clothing for the German army. But...Monsieur Boucher...the only villager charged with that task is Jacques Blanchard, the old sheep farmer. And when he came into the shop earlier this week to deliver the most recent batch of blankets, I asked him if anyone was helping him process the wool. He said no. That he and his granddaughter always worked alone. Just as they had been doing for the past four years." Triumph blazed in her bold, betraying gaze. "Yvette Fleury is up to something. I can feel it in my bones."

Seasoned hunter and expert tracker, Étienne's predatory instincts told him the sneaky snitch was right.

The beguiling beauty with the haunted silvery stare harbored a dark, delicious secret which he was determined to uncover.

Étienne would pluck—one by one—the luscious, forbidden petals of the fragrant flower, Yvette Fleury.

The intriguing, irresistible witch of the enchanted Breton woods.

Chapter 8

A Fateful Encounter

Beau was making great progress in his physical recovery. Yvette often watched him perform his modified calisthenics, admiring his tightly held butt muscles as he kept his injured leg elevated behind him while he did pushups on the pinewood floor. Other times, she marveled at his bulging biceps and gleaming chest muscles while he lifted heavy buckets of empty oyster shells before she ground them up for fertilizer in the garden or returned them to the sandy shore in the sheltered cove. In another week, his fractured bone would be sufficiently healed for her to remove the makeshift cast. But she would continue to wrap the leg for support as Beau began easing weight onto it, walking around inside the cottage, preparing for his inevitable departure.

An ominous future without him that Yvette did not want to confront.

Although his body had nearly returned to normal, his memory had not. He still had only vague recollections of a distant childhood. Playing baseball, climbing trees, seeing snow on the ground…but nothing more. Except the haunting, piercing wail of a female voice. The woman he believed was his mother.

Why was she howling in pain? Beau couldn't remember. Which frustrated him to no end.

Yvette often fretted over the impending future. She couldn't imagine him simply venturing off on his own, even with the splint removed and the strength regained in his leg. How could he possibly rejoin his regiment when he couldn't even remember his own name? He had no idea of his mission, his rank, nor his duty. He didn't know where to report, or how to reunite with his men. Was he their leader? How could he resume military command when he had no idea who he was or what they were supposed to accomplish? Beau simply couldn't set off alone into the woods wearing an American army uniform. The Butcher's men would surely capture him. And, once the Russian Wolfhounds arrived, Beau's chances for escape were nearly impossible. No, that was not a viable option. Yvette had to think of something else. And soon.

She'd considered asking Jules—with his extensive network of contacts within the French Resistance—to arrange for forged documents which would give Beau a new name and established background. But even if they were successful in obtaining falsified identification papers, Beau still wouldn't be able to go into town—or even leave the cottage. Because all strong, young, able-bodied Frenchmen had been conscripted by the Vichy regime—the French government collaborating with the Germans—and sent into forced labor camps. Working in munitions factories, shipyards, or transportation facilities. Plowing fields and harvesting crops to feed the voracious Wehrmacht army. Building Hitler's Atlantic Wall, the two-thousand-mile-long coastal defense of fortresses, gun emplacements, bunkers, and heavy artillery to protect the German forces.

Even if she tried to pass Beau off as a distant cousin, he'd still be compelled to report to a forced labor camp. Where he'd be worked to death like millions of others.

Yvette quickly discarded that implausible idea as well.

No, she'd have to keep Beau here with her, just as she was doing now. He couldn't rejoin his regiment without knowing who he was or where they were. There was no feasible way for him to assume a new identity. And, in her heart, Yvette couldn't bear to see him go.

She knew that fate had brought Beau here. To her. That their destinies had been entwined for a reason which had not yet been revealed.

Yvette knew that they belonged together. And that she'd lost her heart.

To the handsome American soldier with eyes as blue as the Breton sea.

****

One afternoon, as they finished the midday meal together in the kitchen, Beau watched Yvette eat a plump strawberry that she'd picked from the fruit-laden plants in the backyard. His body stirred at the sight of her full, rosebud lips as he envisioned plundering them with his own.

He longed for her all the time. The more often they made love, the more he wanted her. She was utterly irresistible. And he could never get enough.

She was an intriguing, enigmatic blend of contradictions. Pale, creamy complexion, with skin as soft as the tender petals of a rare flower. Fragile, ephemeral, and delicate. Yet—like a rose with sharp, prickly thorns—she was a fighter. A warrior. A survivor.

And a valued member of *les Loups*.

Beau was angry that he had to hide in the cellar each time she went to harvest shellfish at the cove. He wanted to go with her. Help her. Defend her.

Because he knew *la Milice* were everywhere, searching for members of the French Resistance. And the Butcher was determined to capture her brother Jules. The alpha wolf, *Garou*.

Yvette had told him how she'd heard the baker's wife say that the Butcher was traveling to Cancale. To meet with an SS officer who had commandeered a farmhouse on a cliff overlooking the sea.

Yvette's family farm.

Where she'd witnessed the slaughter of her father and brothers by the same Nazis who now lived in her former home.

Beau's gut clenched in frustration and rage.

He was aggravated that his memory had not returned. With hard work over the past few weeks, his body was physically fit and his leg was almost fully healed. Yet, without knowing who he was or why he was here, he couldn't just head blindly into the Breton woods and hope he'd encounter Allied Forces or rejoin his American regiment. It was absurd. He'd much more likely end up in the hands of the Butcher's torturer.

He was as good as dead the moment he walked out Yvette's front door.

And yet, he was restless. Useless. Worthless.

He couldn't go with her to the inlet. Or into town. He couldn't even use the damn outhouse in the backyard. He had to suffer the humiliation of her emptying his filthy chamber pot every day. The frustration and fury was paralyzing.

"It irks me that Madame Dubois came here and looked in my windows." Yvette sipped her cup of chicory, her lips drawn taut with anger. "She's a snoop. An informant. She reports everything to the Butcher. I'm sure she told him how I have bags of fleece. And how I said I was helping a neighbor make blankets for the German army." Yvette glanced at the stack of carded wool in the corner of the room. "Now I'll have to sacrifice a few. Which means I'll have less for *les Loups*."

Like silvery mirrors, her pale blue eyes reflected the fear she desperately tried to hide. "And now, the Butcher will investigate. I'm terrified that I might have compromised Jacques and Lola Blanchard." Tears spilled down her crumpled cheeks. "They're like family to me. Jacques is the nearest thing I've ever had to a grandfather, since I never knew either of my own. He was close to Yanna—my grandmother *Mamie*'s best friend. The kind woman who lived here and took me in when the Nazis killed my family. And Lola—once she marries Jules—will be the sister I never had. I just couldn't bear it if my lie to Marie-Claire Dubois leads the Butcher to them." Despair distorted her bleak gaze. "The German army has no use for the old, the weak, or the sick. Unproductive citizens are unwanted burdens for the Nazi regime. If the Gestapo thinks that Jacques can't produce his required quota of blankets…" Yvette covered her face and sobbed into her hands.

Beau lurched from the table, hopped on one foot to her side, and cradled her over his thundering heart.

She buried her head into his chest and moaned from the pit of her stomach.

Just as he lifted her chin and swallowed her lips with

his own—intending to wash away her pain with waves of passion—the sound of an engine in front of the cottage abruptly halted their amorous embrace.

"Quick—hide in the bedroom. I'll stall whoever it is." Yvette dashed to the window to peer outside. Stark terror shone in her enormous eyes as she spun toward him. "It's the Butcher! Hurry!"

Beau rushed into the bedroom, his pulse hammering in his throat. Yvette wanted him to hide. But he knew why the Butcher was here. Armed with information which jeopardized the ones she loved, he could control Yvette. And force her to submit to his will.

Something Beau would never allow.

So, instead of crawling down into the cellar like a craven coward, he lurked behind the bedroom door, leaving it open just a crack. Limbs shaking with adrenaline, his mouth dry as a bone, Beau watched Yvette open the front door.

And—as the barbarous butcher burst into the quaint stone cottage—waited for the right moment to strike.

"*Bonjour,* Yvette. I'm here to investigate a suspicious report." The Butcher shouldered past her and stormed into the kitchen, just out of Beau's field of vision. "Why are you making stacks of blankets? And where are you getting the fleece? The only local farmer with sheep is Jacques Blanchard. Are you stealing wool that is destined for the German army?"

"No, Monsieur Boucher. I would never do that." Yvette's voice quavered with nervous tension. "I am merely helping a neighbor, that's all." She hovered near the table at the edge of the kitchen, clutching the sides of her blue cotton dress, her head lowered in agitation and supplication.

Beau saw the Butcher amble forward around the side of the table, a sinister sneer stretched across his steely, rigid face. Built like a bull, his menacing bulk slowly approached Yvette's left side. "And would that neighbor happen to be Jacques Blanchard? An elderly farmer who can no longer produce his assigned quota for the Third Reich?" The swine snickered, his vile snout snuffling Yvette's luxurious hair as she trembled in his predatory presence.

Muscles jumping from jolts of adrenaline, Beau seethed as the Butcher stroked Yvette's cheek, gloating in his absolute power over her. "The Nazis have no tolerance for useless old men. If I were to report Jacques Blanchard, the Gestapo would quickly eliminate him. They'd seize his farm. His entire herd of sheep. And his pretty granddaughter? She'd be whisked off to work in a German brothel. Forced to service ten or twenty Nazi soldiers per night. *Unless...*" The Butcher seductively traced his finger down Yvette's throat, over her shaking shoulder, lingering at the swell of her breast. "...you could convince me *not to.*" He fondled the curve of her butt, bunching up the fabric of her dress as he rubbed his jutting pelvis against her rounded hips.

The Butcher flipped Yvette around to face him, pinning her against the table, trapping her between his beefy arms. "Lift your dress, Yvette. Drop your pretty panties. And spread your legs for me. Right here. Right now. Or I'll report Jacques Blanchard to the Gestapo. And you—for stealing bags of wool."

Jaw tightly clenched, pulse pounding in his ears, Beau watched through the crack of the bedroom door as Étienne Boucher unstrapped his holstered pistol and laid it down on the kitchen table. He fumbled with the hem of Yvette's dress, hoisting it up over her hips. Snorting like a rutting hog, he peeled her panties to the floor and lifted her feet out of them. He slammed her back flat against the table and yanked her trembling thighs apart with meaty, greedy hands.

Yvette's panicked face was frozen in fear, her lower lip quivering in abject terror. While tears streamed down her crumpled cheeks, the Butcher unzipped his pants, grunting like a pig as he prepared to mount her.

Beau, ignoring the searing pain in his injured leg, crept silently up from behind.

And—grasping either side of the monstrous nape—snapped the Butcher's fucking neck.

The hefty bulk of Étienne Boucher collapsed in a lifeless heap onto the cold kitchen floor.

Ascertaining that the Butcher was indeed dead, Beau gently smoothed Yvette's dress back down over her shaking legs, helped her step into and pull up her underwear, and enveloped her in comforting, protective arms. "Shhh…it's over. He's dead. He can never hurt you again." Beau cradled Yvette over his thundering heart, rocking her back and forth and kissing her disheveled hair.

"I couldn't stop him…" she stammered, shuddering violently against his chest. "He said he'd report Jacques to the Gestapo…" Inconsolable, Yvette writhed in his arms, sobbing and spluttering on his flannel shirt.

At the sound of heavy footsteps stomping up the stairs, Beau grabbed the Butcher's gun from the holster and pushed Yvette behind him. Pistol extended, prepared to shoot at the anticipated enemy bursting through the front door, Beau was astounded to see Jules, Briac, Pierrick, and Gwilherm storm into the cottage, armed with automatic rifles.

His scarred, stubbled face contorted in fury and fear, Jules quickly scanned the surroundings as his fellow *Loups,* weapons aimed and ready to fire, crept into the hall to inspect the two bedrooms. Wary regard darting from the Butcher's body on the floor to an armed Beau shielding Yvette, Jules lowered his rifle, closed the front door, and exhaled in audible relief. "Thank you for saving my sister." His steely countenance shifted from battle readiness to fraternal concern as he directed his attention to Yvette. "Did the bastard hurt you?"

Still visibly shaking from the traumatic ordeal, she stepped out from behind Beau on wobbly, unsteady legs. "No, thank God. Beau stopped him. He broke his neck."

Dark gaze glinting with gratitude and respect, Jules bowed his head in acknowledgment to Beau. "Thank you for killing him. I've been trying to. *For years.*" He laid his rifle on the table and wrapped his arms around Yvette while his companions exited the hall and stood watch by the front door. "Briac—from his lookout perch in the tree—saw the Butcher's car coming up the road. We got here as fast as we could." Jules nestled Yvette against his chest, resting his chin upon her head, enclosing her in long, lanky arms.

For a few moments, she lingered in his loving embrace, then stepped back to look up at him with wild, terrified eyes. "The Butcher knew about the wool and the blankets. He threatened to report Jacques and Lola. And Jules…" Yvette clutched her brother's hands, rubbing her thumbs over the scarred, scraped knuckles. "He recently met with an SS Officer in Cancale. At a commandeered farmhouse. *On a cliff overlooking the sea.*" Horror paled her haunted face. "The same Nazi who gunned you down. And killed Papa, Jeffroi, and Jean-Michel." She bent to kiss his calloused hands. "I left a note for you under the rock. At the mouth of the cave." Imploring eyes searched Jules' implacable scowl. "I wanted to warn you. Because the reason the Butcher went to Cancale…was to requisition three dozen Soviet soldiers. To aid *la Milice* in hunting *les Loups.*" Her frail voice faltered and broke as she delivered the dire warning.

"We need to get rid of the body and the car. *Now*. Before anyone sees." Briac joined them in the kitchen, his brows furrowed in a pensive frown. "We'll carve up his fucking face with the wolf paw. Mark his death as a victory for *les Loups.*" He spun to Pierrick and Gwilherm, still guarding the entrance door. "If we leave the body near the village, it'll look like he never made it here. That will clear Yvette of any suspicion. They'll find the corpse…see the wolf mark…and assume we got to him first."

Gwilherm nodded, tugging on his shaggy beard as he contemplated strategy. "We'll load him into the car. Drive back toward the village. Turn the vehicle around— so it looks like he was headed this way. I'll slash the rear tire and open the trunk. As if he stopped to change a flat. And was ambushed by *les Loups* at the edge of the woods."

With a jut of his chin, Jules indicated the Butcher's body as he gave orders to Pierrick and Gwilherm. "Get him in the car. We'll carve him up later—when we stop along the side of the road. I don't want any blood here in the cottage."

As the men complied, a solemn Briac approached Beau. "The Allies have taken Cherbourg and the

Cotentin Peninsula. They're expected to break through the barrier at Avranches any day now. And when they do, they'll be heading west into Brittany. *Les Loups*—like the rest of the Free French Forces—will join them in fighting the Nazis. As we retake vital seaports along Hitler's Atlantic Wall."

Jules clasped Beau's shoulder. "You may not remember your name, but you can still fight with us." He retrieved his weapon from the table, displaying it proudly. "We stole these from the Germans. MP 40 submachine guns. The Allies call them *Schmeissers*. Easy to use. And—since the stock folds up—easy to carry, too." He quickly demonstrated how to operate and load the weapon, handing the gun and an additional magazine of ammunition to Beau. "You keep this. We have others. When the Allies arrive in Brittany—reports indicate they'll be here in two weeks—we'll come back for you. So you can join us in the Battle of Saint-Malo." He smiled sadly at Yvette, whose pale blue gaze glimmered with unshed tears. "Until then, take good care of my sister. We'll be back for you soon."

He shook Beau's hand, as did Briac. The two men hugged Yvette one last time, kissing her cheeks with *la bise* of farewell. And—desperate longing and unwavering love in their loyal lupine eyes—left the cottage.

Climbed into the Butcher's dark green *Citroën*.

And drove off through the Breton woods.

Chapter 9

Memories

The white curtains with tiny blue wildflowers ruffled in the summer breeze, the briny scent of the nearby sea wafting into the sunlit kitchen as Yvette unwrapped Beau's leg and finally removed the splints.

With a sigh of pleasure, he flexed his foot, rotated his ankle, and rose from the wooden chair where he was seated at the oak table. Easing his weight onto his left leg, he stood for a moment on both feet and flashed Yvette a heart-melting grin. "It feels good to stand on two legs again. I am so sick of those damned crutches." With cautious steps, he walked around the kitchen, stopping to rise up onto his toes and bend at the knees before returning triumphantly to Yvette's side. He pulled her close, wrapping his arms around her waist and leaning down to kiss her softly. "Thank you for healing me."

From the burled walnut radio sitting on the kitchen counter, the plaintive, melodic voice of Édith Piaf floated into the air. Placing one of Yvette's hands upon his shoulder, Beau clutched the other, rocking her gently as *la Môme* sang heartfelt words of love.

It was heaven to be enveloped in his sinewy arms, her head nestled against his broad chest. Yvette buried her nose into the tuft of dark hair at the base of his throat, inhaling his scent deep into her lungs. Every pore in her body tingled at his touch as he swayed her slowly across the kitchen floor.

Soon, he'd be gone forever. She couldn't imagine life without him. The penetrating eyes that pierced her soul, the dazzling smile that lit up her lonely life, the beloved body that filled her empty depths and made her shattered spirit soar. Now that she'd touched him…tasted him…melded with him as they became one…how could she ever survive as only half of the whole?

She'd planned to keep him here with her, hidden from the Germans. Filled her foolish heart with hope that they could elude the inevitable future. The unbearable, impossible goodbye.

But now, *les Loups* would return soon. And Beau would leave her behind.

The weight of sorrow was smothering.

Yvette pressed her cheek over his pounding heart, vowing to savor every last moment together. And fill her soul with a fountain of memories to last a lifetime of loneliness without him.

As if he could read her thoughts, he lowered his full lips to swallow hers. Parting them with his skilled tongue, he probed and plundered, sending waves of pleasure to ignite her inner core.

And make her swoon with want.

For the first time without crutches, he led her to the inviting bed. And lavished her, body and soul. The impending separation sparked their passion, and their coupling was primal and raw. When he erupted in volcanic release, pouring himself into her with liquid flames, Yvette clenched him inside and out, drawing his essence deep into hers.

With the painful future looming like an ominous dark cloud on the horizon, they clung all the more desperately to each other. Made love each morning to the trills of alouette songbirds. Savored the flavor of each other's bodies every night, basking in soft moonlight glow. Soared through waves of exquisite bliss to seal forever upon their souls.

"I love you, Yvette." Beau stroked her cheek, gently pushing a tendril away from her lashes. Sensuous mouth brushing hers, he whispered into her parted lips. "If I survive this bloody war, I'll come back to you. I promise."

She cupped the back of his head, pulling him down into a kiss, twirling her tongue with his. Her hands rove over his muscled back, and she slid her body underneath him. Opening her legs and wrapping them around his waist, she rubbed her moist, silky flesh against his hardened length.

With a guttural groan, he impaled her. Pounded her like thunderous surf crashing against the shore. And, as she clutched him in the throes of climax, emptied his soul into hers.

****

Even though she'd been expecting it, when the distinctive pattern of knocks upon her front door signaled the return of *les Loups* two weeks later in the still of the night, Yvette's heart leapt to her throat.

And flew right out of her chest.

Hand shaking, legs trembling, she opened the door to the familiar, beloved faces of her brother and his three closest friends. But with them were two strangers.

American soldiers.

With the same dark blue emblem she'd seen on Beau's uniform.

Two capital letter A's—in the form of a parachute—inside a blue circle on a red square.

And the word Airborne, embroidered in white letters, centered across the top.

As Jules whisked them through the front door and into the cottage, one of the Americans—a stocky, gruff soldier with dark brown hair—spotted Beau standing in the living room with Yvette. Stunned, frozen in disbelief, his mouth dropped open in astonishment as recognition sparked in his widened eyes. "Zach! Thank God, you're alive!"

The other American removed his helmet and wiped a sweaty, grimy brow. Tall and lanky, with sandy brown hair and a prominent nose, he grinned from ear to ear as he beheld Beau. "Man, are you a sight for sore eyes. We've been looking for you for two months. Have you been here the whole time?"

As Beau stood immobile, his brows furrowed in confusion, the dark-haired soldier rushed forward to grasp him by the shoulders. "What's the matter, Zach? Don't you recognize me? I'm Mac. Sergeant Thomas McGuire, 82nd Airborne, 507th PIR, from St. Louis."

"And I'm Murph. Corporal Robert Murphy, from Cleveland. Zach—don't you remember? You're First Lieutenant Richard Zachford. Our squad leader for *Mission Boston*."

****

Memories crashed into Zach, inundating him like the overflowing banks of a raging, roaring river.

He was Richard Zachford, from Kittery, Maine. He

worked in the naval shipyard near Portsmouth, New Hampshire. Lived with his parents—Harold and Dorothy—and his older brother, Walter.

Dad and Walt died in Pearl Harbor. That's why Mom wailed when she heard the news on the radio. And that's why I enlisted. To fight the bastards who killed them. Mom died in the winter of '42. Of pneumonia. And a broken heart.

He remembered everything.

Playing baseball in the empty field with Walt and the guys. Going to Fenway Park to see the Boston Red Sox. Ted Williams—"The Splendid Splinter"—hitting thirty-one homers in 1939. Joining the army. Combat drills in Louisiana. Paratrooper training in California. Preparing in England for Operation Overlord.

D-Day.

The Allied invasion of Normandy.

The jarring predawn flight. Deafening thunder. Nonstop detonations of German flak antiaircraft cannons. The plane getting hit. The forced jump into the black void of hell. The horrendous storm. Gale force winds blowing him right at the looming forest, visible through flashes of lightning. The parachute getting tangled in branches of the huge oak tree. Struggling to get free, his left foot caught in the cords. Plunging headfirst, in an upside down freefall, hanging precariously by one leg. The loud, sickening snap of the tibia bone as it broke like a thick branch of the tree.

And the gut-wrenching, blinding pain as his head exploded, slammed like a slab against the massive, unyielding trunk.

Then nothing. Until now.

Seeing Mac and Murph brought it all back.

He was First Lieutenant Richard Zachford, 82nd Airborne Division, 507th PIR. Parachute Infantry Regiment. *Raff's Ruffians*. Named after their commander, Colonel Edison Raff.

Their regiment was to be dropped onto Utah Beach. Their assignment—Mission Boston—was to secure the Merderet River crossings and pave the way for the Allies to retake the Cotentin Peninsula. And the crucial deep-sea port of Cherbourg, vital for the naval invasion of Normandy.

Operation Neptune.

In a matter of seconds, Zach processed the deluge of overwhelming memories as he stood transfixed, shaking with emotion, staring at the relieved, grinning faces of his two brothers-in-arms.

"Please, come in. And sit at the table." Yvette ushered the soldiers into the kitchen and nodded to Jules. "You and Briac—bring the extra chairs from the bedrooms and set them here around the table. I'll fix you a quick meal. Are you hungry?"

"Starved. But we can't stay long. We need to move out tonight. While it's still dark." Jules kissed his sister's two cheeks, as did Briac, Pierrick, and Gwilherm. He and Briac returned with two extra chairs each, settling into the wooden seats around the oak table along with the other men.

A stunned, speechless Zach stared incredulously at the two grinning American soldiers.

Yvette served everyone a cup of chicory, returning to the stove to scramble eggs with fresh herbs, mushrooms, and *brebis* cheese.

The dark-haired soldier, Mac, gratefully accepted the mug she offered, took a large gulp, and spoke to

Zach. "When our plane got hit, we had to jump. But it was way too soon. We were supposed to get dropped onto Utah Beach, but we never made it that far. Some of the men—weighed down by the heavy gear—drowned in the marsh. The Germans had flooded the plain near the Douve River, to stop us. But it backfired, because they couldn't reinforce their Wehrmacht army, either. Or get their Panzer tanks through. The Nazis tried to prevent us from consolidating Omaha and Utah beaches. It took a week of bloody hell, but thank God, we won the Battle of Carentan. And linked the two American beachheads, securing the base for the rest of the Allied landings."

Yvette set a platter of cheese, wild plums, and bread in the center of the table, with a plate of herb-seasoned eggs and mushrooms in front of each man. Famished, they dug in, and she sat down beside Zach to join them.

"We took Cherbourg at the end of June, and the rest of the Cotentin Peninsula in the first couple weeks of July. Mac and I left Avranches two days ago. The Allies are going to push through there any day now, moving west as part of Operation Cobra. The Battle of Brittany. To reclaim the vital seaports along the Breton coast. Our new mission is to capture the port of Saint-Malo. And drive the Germans out of the channel island of *Cézembre*." The sandy-haired Murph cleaned his plate, sopping up the juices with a large hunk of *pain de campagne*. He popped the nutty, herb-laced bread into his mouth and grinned gratefully at Yvette. "That was delicious. Thank you, ma'am. *Merci beaucoup*."

English was his native language, but it sounded foreign to Zach after two solid months of hearing and speaking nothing but French.

Yvette, Jules, and Briac spoke some English, but

Gwilherm and Pierrick did not. And since neither Mac nor Murph spoke much French, Zach served as translator for his American friends and *les Loups.*

"Zach—I saw you get blown into the woods. We searched all day but found nothing. Except your dog tags." Mac handed him the stainless-steel identification badge, attached to a metal chain, which Zach placed around his neck and tucked under his shirt. "What happened? How'd you end up here? Were you injured?"

"Yvette found me." Zach reached for the hand she'd placed in her lap and gave it a grateful squeeze. "My parachute got all tangled up in the branches of a tree. I was hanging upside down, suspended from one leg. She got Jules and *les Loups* here…" He gestured to the men seated at the table. "…to cut the strings and lower me to the ground."

Zach raised Yvette's fingers to his lips and held her pale blue gaze, the love-light in her shining eyes a beacon for his adrift soul. "Yvette's a gifted healer. An herbalist who practices natural medicine." He chuckled softly and smiled at the woman he loved. "With all her potions, ointments, and elixirs—the local villagers call her *the Witch of the Breton Woods.*"

Yvette leaned forward to address the two American soldiers. "Beau's—I mean Zach's—leg was badly broken, and he had a serious head injury. In fact, he's been suffering from amnesia for the past two months. Until tonight, when the sight of the two of you made his memories return." She dazzled Zach with a glorious smile that took his breath away.

"Well, thank God she found you and not the Germans." Mac drained his cup of chicory and wiped his mouth with a swarthy hand.

"Or *la Milice*—the paramilitary bastards that collaborate with the Nazis." Murph shared a wicked, conspiratorial grin with Mac. "We took out quite a few of them along the way."

"There are about thirty-five thousand members of the French Resistance scattered throughout Bretagne. *Les Forces Françaises de l' Intérieur*—the FFI. Bands of clandestine groups—*les Maquis*—hiding in the woods like us," Jules said to the Americans as he handed his empty plate to Yvette. "The FFI receives supply drops from the Allies—ammunition, radio sets, explosives, food rations—so we can sabotage the Germans. We've already destroyed some of the railroad tracks the Nazis use to transport equipment and ammunition. With the coded messages we receive from the BBC, the FFI knows when and where to strike."

"Intelligence reports indicate that there are close to ten thousand Germans garrisoned at the port of Saint-Malo—a designated fortress of Hitler's Atlantic Wall. We plan to join the Allied infantry units converging there. To capture the citadel and the nearby channel island of *Cézembre*. We're heading out tonight." Briac nodded to Zach. "You need to wear your American uniform. Grab your gear and get ready to go. We can't linger here."

Zach's heart clenched as he met Yvette's anguished gaze. In her haunted, silvery eyes, he glimpsed the same despair that gripped his throat in a smothering vice. How could he possibly leave her?

The men rose from the table and gathered their weapons, preparing to depart.

Jules removed a pistol from the holster strapped at his waist and handed it to Yvette. "This is an FP-45

Liberator. The barrel is only four inches long, so it'll fit it in the palm of your hand. It's got a silencer and a safety." He demonstrated how to disengage and reconnect the safety. "It only fires one shot at close range. Use it only as a last resort."

She examined the gun in her hand as Jules continued. "After we leave, it's essential that you follow your normal daily routine. Don't deviate in any way. You know nothing about the Butcher's death. You're unaware that Marie-Claire Dubois betrayed you. Because the Butcher never came here." He hugged her tight, his deep voice gravelly as he cradled her in his sinewy arms. "Arouse no suspicion. Continue exactly as you did before."

Blinking back tears, she nodded against his wiry chest, then withdrew from her brother's embrace to take hold of Zach's hand. Her forlorn expression implored Jules as she led Zach toward the bedroom door. "Five minutes. Please. To say goodbye."

His disgruntled scowl was a disapproving grimace, but he ducked his chin in reluctant agreement. "Hurry. We need to leave."

****

Zach closed the bedroom door and pulled Yvette close, wrapping his arms behind her. He devoured her lips with a desperate, frantic kiss. "I remember everything. My mother's cry…was because my dad and brother were killed in Pearl Harbor." He kissed her hands, a lump of grief constricting his throat. "I couldn't ask you before, because I couldn't remember the past. But now I do…and I know that I don't have a wife or kids back home. Yvette, if I survive this damn war and come back to you…will you marry me?"

She flung her arms around his neck with a whimper of joy, rising onto her tiptoes to whisper into his mouth. "Yes, I will marry you, Beau...*Zach*. But you must promise to come back to me."

He chuckled softly as he held her against his chest. "I'm Zach to everyone else. But to you...I want you to always call me Beau. I love that name. Because you gave it to me." He dipped her back in his arms and plundered her mouth, swallowing her lips and sharing her rasping breath. "I promise to try my best to stay alive. I love you, Yvette Fleury. My beautiful witch of the Breton woods."

Zach stood her up, withdrew from her arms, and crossed the room. He moved the bed, lifted the hidden panel, and lowered himself down into the cellar. Hoisting his gear onto the bedroom floor, he pulled himself back up, replaced the wooden plank, and repositioned the bed. Donning his uniform, helmet, boots, and backpack, he slung the MP 40 submachine gun that Jules had given him over his shoulder.

With one final embrace, he said goodbye to Yvette and opened the bedroom door, leading her back into the living room where the waiting men stood ready to leave.

Yvette hugged Mac and Murph, then kissed each of *les Loups* with a tearful French *bise* of goodbye. She clung to her brother and caressed his bristled cheek. "Come back to us, Jules. You promised to marry Lola. Stay alive for her. And for me."

His fierce lupine gaze glimmered with grief. "You stay alive, too. *Je t'aime, ma petite soeur*. I love you, my little sister."

Briac hustled the group out the front door.

With one last desperate kiss for her, Zach followed the soldiers down the exterior steps.

Brimming with tears, Yvette watched the man who took her heart with him as he headed off into the dense Breton woods.

But she smiled despite her debilitating pain, her hand resting protectively on her lower stomach.

Because Beau had left a part of himself behind.

Nestled safely in her loving womb.

Chapter 10

Storm Surge

Obersturmführer Heinrich Balsch stood near the mahogany table in the office of his commandeered farmhouse, contemplating the turbulent sea crashing against the craggy cliff of *la Côte d' Émeraude*—the Emerald Coast of Brittany. Stymied by the unexpected turn of recent events, he gazed pensively out the large windows, methodically examining the bits of information which fit together like an intricate jigsaw puzzle.

With one baffling piece still missing.

The Russian Cossack soldiers had arrived as expected at the local train station. He'd assigned a dozen of the former Soviet prisoners to prepare for a vital mission in the village of *le Vivier-Sur-Mer.* Requisitioning a transport truck, experienced driver, and ammunition, Heinrich had amassed everything that Étienne Boucher would need to hunt down the *maquis*—the radical members of the French Resistance hiding in the dense Breton woods.

The dangerous, destructive, and deadly band who called themselves *les Loups.*

Yet, despite his impeccable record for punctuality and inimitable service to the Third Reich, Section Leader

Étienne Boucher had not come to Cancale on July 20th for his scheduled appointment to receive the *Russian Wolfhounds*. Nor had he called to inform Heinrich of an unanticipated delay.

He simply hadn't shown up. Totally inconsistent with his exemplary performance and untarnished reputation.

When Heinrich's secretary had called Étienne Boucher's office to inquire about the missed appointment, he'd learned that the Section Leader of *la Milice* had been murdered. The grotesquely mutilated corpse had been found next to Boucher's prized green *Citroën,* along the side of the road near the village of *le Vivier-Sur-Mer*. From all outward appearances, he'd stopped to change a flat tire at the edge of the forest and had been ambushed.

As if he'd been attacked by a pack of wolves, Boucher's lacerated face had been viciously slashed by sharp claws.

The unequivocal mark of the rabid Resistance rebels who called themselves *les Loups.*

Heinrich had subsequently sent four of his most efficient SS men to investigate.

They'd interrogated the members of *la Milice* who'd worked for Étienne Boucher, as well as several villagers redeeming ration coupons in the local supply store. An informant named Marie-Claire Dubois had notified his men that Section Leader Boucher had gone to investigate a suspicious report of a local woman—Yvette Fleury—stealing bags of wool destined for the Wehrmacht army. She'd been allegedly using the stolen fleece to make unauthorized, undocumented stacks of blankets.

Heinrich's unerring instincts told him that this

woman was somehow connected to Étienne Boucher's death.

And undoubtedly linked to *les Loups.*

A week after his men had returned from *le Vivier-Sur-Mer* with the intelligence reports about Section Leader Boucher's mysterious murder, the railroad tracks along the Atlantic Coast leading to Cancale had been destroyed by French Resistance forces.

Preventing the delivery of the Tiger tanks, artillery, explosives, and ammunition that Heinrich needed to reinforce and defend the ten miles of Cancale coastline for the impending, anticipated Battle of Saint-Malo.

Two nights ago, the dozen guards patrolling his garrison had been killed—their necks snapped and faces slashed with the same wolf marks found on Étienne Boucher. Five of the ten barracks that Heinrich had constructed to house his regiment had also been destroyed, the buildings on the eastern peninsular point decimated, as Nazi soldiers died in the insidious, incendiary blaze caused by a string of sudden explosions. Fortunately, the five buildings on the western side of the property had been spared, the enemy detonation devices failing—perhaps due to recent rains.

Shaking with fury, Heinrich Balsch contemplated the thunderous surf which echoed his tumultuous rage.

The Resistance bastards had murdered Étienne Boucher. Blown up the train tracks along the Breton coast. Prevented delivery of tanks and ammunition necessary to defend the Führer's Atlantic Wall.

The vile vermin had destroyed half of his garrison, killing two hundred and fifty exemplary Nazi soldiers and a dozen loyal, highly competent guards.

His fortification had been decimated—and very

nearly demolished—by the rabid wolves of the French Resistance.

Les Loups.

At the sound of precise, measured bootsteps marching down the hall, Heinrich diverted his attention from the savage Breton sea to the impeccably dressed SS Officer standing in military salute at the entrance to the room.

His personal secretary, *Leutnant* Hans Müller.

"Forgive the intrusion, *Herr Obersturmführer.*" Müller's deferential tone conveyed utmost respect as he strode briskly across the room. "But a message has arrived from Gestapo Headquarters in Paris with the information you requested from the *Carlingue.*" He handed the official communiqué to Heinrich with a deferential nod.

"*Danke.*" Heinrich opened the sealed envelope and read the names of the French family who had originally inhabited this commandeered farmhouse, along with the dates of their births and—for the deceased—their deaths.

When he reached the bottom of the list, every hair on the back of Heinrich's neck stood on end. Chills ran up his spine. Goose bumps prickled his flesh.

He now knew the identity of the son who had miraculously survived the Nazi shooting.

The one who had escaped into the forest.

The wounded victim saved by the French Resistance rabble.

The alpha wolf *Garou,* leader of *les Loups,* was Jules Fleury.

But—in a delightfully unexpected surprise—Heinrich had also discovered that the young woman with the suspicious bags of stolen wool and mysterious stacks of blankets that Étienne Boucher had gone to investigate was *Garou*'s younger sister.

Obersturmführer Balsch glanced out the window at the turbulent surf, thrilled to have found the missing puzzle piece. He now had the means to trap the alpha wolf, foil the French Resistance, and avenge the heinous death of his stalwart men. "Summon the four SS Officers I recently sent to *le Vivier-Sur-Mer*. The ones who investigated Section Leader Boucher's mysterious murder. I have a new assignment for them. A valuable prisoner to be brought to me for interrogation."

Heinrich shot Müller a cunning, wicked grin.

"Yvette Fleury. *The Witch of the Breton Woods*."

Chapter 11

Le Pardon de Sainte Anne

After Beau's departure, Yvette continued with her usual routine, like Jules had insisted. Twice a week, she arose before dawn to collect shellfish at the cove, the fatigue of early pregnancy making the four-mile trek hauling the wagon much more physically difficult. The pungent tang of the briny seafood aggravated her constant nausea, often resulting in an unavoidable stop as she emptied the contents of her stomach along the way.

Each time she bartered with the baker's wife, Marie-Claire Dubois, Yvette cringed under the suspicious glare of the hateful woman who had betrayed her. But since Yvette could not reveal any knowledge of the Butcher's death, she did her best to maintain a cool composure, as if nothing had changed between them.

Today, as Yvette approached the dreaded stone cottage, the traitorous snitch stepped out her front door, wiping her hands on a soiled white apron. Her disdainful mouth was puckered into an ugly grimace of contempt and disapproval. "What do you have for me today?" Madame Dubois stepped down the three stone stairs, walking over to inspect Yvette's hand-drawn wooden wagon.

"The tide wasn't right for clams or scallops, but I do have some lovely mussels." Yvette pulled back the blanket which covered the bucket of seafood, battling a sudden wave of nearly incapacitating nausea. *I can't vomit in front of her. She might think I have a contagious illness and refuse to barter with me. And I need the corn for my hens.* "They're small—which means they'll be tender and sweet."

Madame Dubois harrumphed. "I don't care for mussels. But Marcel likes them. Wait here while I fetch your supplies."

While the baker's wife brought the mussels inside, Yvette dashed to the edge of the woods and hurled the bile from her stomach into the wildflowers which lined the dirt path. Pretending that she'd been admiring the purple and pink heather blooms, she wiped her mouth inconspicuously and returned to the wagon just as Madame Dubois came out of the cottage.

The leery informant handed Yvette the sacks of grain and two loaves of *pain de campagne*. Eager to share vicious, scathing gossip, she leaned toward Yvette, her fetid breath fouling the fresh air. "Four SS Officers came into the bakery a few days ago, asking lots of questions. They're investigating Étienne Boucher's murder. Did you know his body was found beside his car, just outside the village? His face had been carved by the wolf claw—the distinctive trademark of *les Loups*." Madame Dubois' beady, vermin eyes followed Yvette's every move as she loaded the flour, oats, and corn into the back of her wagon, trying not to show her distress. "Didier Chauvin has been appointed as new Section Leader of *la Milice*. He has sworn to work with the Gestapo—and the Russian Wolfhounds who recently arrived in Cancale—to track down those rabid, rebel wolves. The Nazis will find them. Torture them for information. And eliminate every last one of *les Loups*."

Yvette's legs were shaking. Marie-Claire Dubois had undoubtedly informed the investigating SS Officers of the suspicious report of stolen wool that she had made to the Butcher. Perhaps she'd also told them that he'd been on his way to Yvette's cottage when he'd been killed. *Relax. Jules said to continue exactly as before. I can't show any apprehension. I know nothing about the Butcher's death.* Swallowing her trepidation, Yvette smiled weakly and nodded. "I'm sure you're right. Well—I must get home, to put these mussels into the icebox. Good day, Madame Dubois. *Bonne journée."*

Pulling the wooden wagon behind her, Yvette trudged along the dirt path at the edge of the woods. She couldn't wait to see Jacques and Lola Blanchard.

To help dispel her gnawing fear that the Nazis were closing in.

****

"*Bonjour,* Yvette. *Papi* went into town to deliver the blankets and pick up a few supplies." Lola kissed both of Yvette's cheeks with an affectionate smile. "Want to come in for a cup of chicory?"

"Not today, thanks. I'm feeling pretty queasy, and I think the chicory would upset my stomach. Maybe next time?" Yvette accepted the wheel of *brebis* cheese and containers of sheep milk, loading them into the back of the wagon.

Her pulse hammered in her throat as she met Lola's concerned gaze. "Marie-Claire Dubois just informed me that SS Officers were in town a few days ago, investigating the Butcher's death. From the claw marks on his face, they know he was killed by *les Loups*." Yvette clutched Lola's hands, her own shaking uncontrollably. "Didier Chauvin is the new head of *la Milice*. The Russian Wolfhounds have arrived, and now—with the Gestapo involved in investigating the Butcher's murder—I'm terrified they'll trap Jules and *les Loups*."

Large brown eyes brimming with tears, Lola hugged her tight. "I know. Me, too. But we must believe they'll make it safely to Saint-Malo. Before the Nazis find them."

Somewhat assuaged by her friend's comforting embrace and sage advice, Yvette retrieved a bucket of mussels from the back of her wagon and handed it to Lola. "You're right. We must have faith. Please give Jacques a big hug for me. I'm sorry I missed him. See you Saturday."

"*À bientôt.* See you soon." Lola kissed Yvette's cheeks with *la bise* of goodbye.

And Yvette, trailing her wagon laden with bartered goods, returned home to her cozy cottage in the woods.

****

After storing the seafood, cheese, and milk in the icebox, Yvette intended to lie down for a rest when she heard the unmistakable low rumble of a car engine. Panicked, she peered out the front window.

And nearly fainted at the sight of a black sedan with swastika flags flapping in the wind.

She raced into the bedroom, grabbed the pistol Jules had given her, and tucked it into the waistband of her pants. Pushing aside the bed, she popped open the hidden panel in the floor and lowered her legs into the opening. Bending at the waist and supporting her weight on one arm, she suspended herself on her stomach, pulling the covering back into place and dropping down onto the ground inside the cellar. Panting and shaking, she crawled on the earthen floor within the foundation, scrabbling up behind the supportive column to hide from view.

Please don't let them find me. I don't want my baby to die.

Amid heavy stomping and the scraping of furniture being hauled across the floor, Yvette trembled violently as angry, booming male voices shouted her name. "Yvette Fleury! *Zeigen Sie sich!* Show yourself!"

A sudden, sharp staccato of gunshots made Yvette's stomach leap to her throat.

Paralyzed with terror, she was dumfounded to hear the distinctive pattern of knocks on the floor above her head. Through the opened panel, Lola's lilting voice floated like a melody to her stunned, incredulous ears. "Yvette, It's Lola and *Papi*. It's safe to come up now."

Limbs still trembling, Yvette stood on weakened legs, brushing off her knees to calm her ragged nerves. In the dark, loamy dirt of the cellar floor, a glint of reflected light caught her eye. She bent down to retrieve the object, surprised to find a metal vial with the word *penicillin* written on a label affixed to the front.

I have never heard of this, but it appears to be medicine. It must have fallen out of Beau's backpack. I'll put it my satchel, with the herbal tinctures and ointments. If—no, when—I see him again, I'll give it back.

Yvette tucked the tube inside her bra and staggered across the ground within the cellar.

Through the sunny opening in the bedroom floor, Lola's glowing face shone like an angel from above.

Smiling with obvious relief, she reached down to Yvette. "Here, take my hand. I'll pull you up."

Yvette grasped the proffered hand and, with Lola's help, hoisted herself up onto the pinewood floor. She clutched her friend in a desperate hug. "What happened? I heard gunshots."

"*Papi* used the MP 40 that Jules gave him. Four SS men were here in the cottage to arrest you." Lola comforted a still-shaking Yvette as Jacques, carrying the grayish green visored hat of a German uniform—with the infamous *totenkopf* death skull insignia on the black leather band—marched into the room.

"Lola and I will haul the bodies out of the cottage and into the woods. Yvette—wipe up the blood on the floor as best you can, and pull the rug over to cover the stain. Pack a change of clothes and grab your bag of herbal supplies. We'll steal the car and ditch it in Cherrueix. There's a religious parade and festival today. Hundreds of people will be celebrating in the streets— with music, dancing, and food. We'll evade the Germans by mingling with the villagers. And inside the chapel, we're meeting an old friend of mine who'll drive us to Saint-Malo."

Yvette's heart froze. *That's where Beau, Jules, and les Loups have gone. To fight ten thousand Germans!* "We're going to Saint-Malo?" Her voice cracked as her throat went dry.

"We can't fight in the battle beside our men. But we can certainly volunteer as nurses to care for the injured in the American hospital there. You're a skilled healer. And *Papi* and I can bandage wounds. Come, we must hurry. More Nazis might be on the way." Lola dashed into the living room to help her grandfather carry the first of four slain SS Officers out of the cottage and into the nearby woods.

Yvette stood transfixed in the bedroom doorway, staring at the corpses and blood scattered across the wooden floor.

Gruesome memories of her father and brothers being gunned down by Nazis flooded her in a numbing wave of horror.

As she gaped at the mutilated victims, Lola and Jacques returned to retrieve another body. The touch of Lola's hand on the small of her back spurred Yvette into action.

She dashed into the bedroom to fetch several towels, returning to mop up blood and gore from the floor. The coppery stench turned her stomach, but she held her breath to staunch the nausea, covering a dark stain with Yanna's favorite braided rug. She stuffed the ruined linens into empty buckets, carrying them outside to dump in the woods near the soldiers' bodies.

"If anyone looks through your windows, everything will appear normal inside the cottage. It'll take a while for the Nazis to find these bodies, giving us time to escape." Jacques wiped his sweaty brow, inhaled deeply, and turned toward Yvette as he donned the German military hat. "Ready to go?"

"I just need to grab my bag. And the pistol Jules gave me. Be right back." While Jacques and Lola got in the car, Yvette dashed into the cottage, grabbed her satchel of herbs, and slipped the tube of penicillin into a small pouch inside the leather bag. She checked the safety on the small pistol Jules had given her and tucked the weapon inside her bra. Stuffing a change of clothes into her large purse, she slung her satchel of herbs over her shoulder. Racing out the front door, she stopped to lock it, then sprinted to the running car. As soon as she climbed into the back seat, Jacques, wearing the distinctive, visored hat of a *Waffen-SS* Nazi Officer, sped the stolen vehicle away from the stone cottage.

Yvette took a deep breath and exhaled slowly, trying to slow her racing heart. She leaned forward from the back seat to speak to Jacques. "How did you know the Nazis were in my cottage?"

"When I went into the village this morning to deliver the blankets, there were four SS men in the supply store, investigating the Butcher's death. I overheard them ask the shopkeeper where you lived, informing him that you were a suspect wanted for interrogation. I raced home to get the MP 40, and Lola fetched the key that you had given her for emergencies. I snuck into the kitchen through the back door and fired upon them from behind." Jacques' sage, crinkled gaze met hers in the rearview mirror. "I'm a former soldier, you know. I fired machine guns in World War I."

As they barreled down the bumpy dirt road, another black sedan with swastika flags passed them, headed in the opposite direction.

Toward the cottage.

"*Papi*—there were four Nazi officers in that car. *They saw us*," Lola whispered hoarsely as she watched the car retreat from view.

"They'll most likely radio their commander in Cancale. The SS Officer that the Butcher met with to requisition the Russian Wolfhounds. The one who sent them here to investigate Étienne Boucher's death." Jacques scowled, his brows furrowed pensively.

A ripple of horror shivered up Yvette's spine.

The same monster who gunned down Papa, Jeffroi, Jean-Michel, and Jules.

She swallowed hard as bitter bile rose in her gut.

"They probably know that you have long, black hair. Braid it, and tuck it up under this. You'll be less likely to attract attention." Lola handed Yvette a blue bandana.

Yvette nodded. "Good idea." She plaited her thick, dark curls and secured the strands on top of her head, hiding her hair under the cotton scarf.

"There's a vehicle inspection checkpoint at the intersection leading into Cherrueix. We'll take a side road to avoid that. I know a restaurant where we can leave the car and walk into town from there. With all the revelry for *Le Pardon de Sainte Anne*—the religious parade for today's festival—we'll be able to join the procession and make our way to the chapel." Jacques veered off the main boulevard, took a series of side turns down narrow, empty streets, and parked the black sedan near a bistro which was closed for the holiday celebration.

The three of them exited the car, and Jacques tossed the German hat on the driver's seat inside the vehicle. With a deep intake of breath, he smiled reassuringly at Yvette and Lola. Offering an elbow to each, he escorted them up the hill, along the sidewalk, and into the picturesque village of Cherrueix.

****

Along the main cobblestone street of the quaint seaside town, bagpipes, flutes, and violins filled the brisk Breton air with vibrant strands of Celtic music under the clear, cerulean summer sky. Women clad in the traditional costume of long black dresses adorned with white lace collars, aprons, and elaborate *coiffes*—tall, intricately woven headpieces—danced *la gavotte* with men in black hats, white shirts, embroidered vests, and dark pants. Despite the limited food supplies due to war rations, the sizzling seafood aroma of clams, cockles, mussels, and shrimp mingled with the sweet scents of cinnamon and chocolate of the *crêpes* and salty *galettes*—the thin pancakes which were a specialty of the regional cuisine.

With the religious procession called *le pardon,* villagers paid tribute to Sainte Anne, mother of the Virgin Mary and patron saint of *la Bretagne*, credited with sparing the lives of those in peril. Sailors rescued from shipwrecks carried sections of wood from their salvaged vessels. Former cripples displayed the crutches they no longer needed to walk. Victims who escaped a fire carried the rope which saved them from flames as the parade meandered from the center of town to the stone chapel near the salty marsh where seagrass swayed in the briny breeze.

Despite the joyous revelry, Yvette's heart leapt to her throat at the sight of armed Nazi soldiers circulating among the townspeople, scrutinizing the crowd with merciless, malevolent stares.

"We need to split up. The car that passed us might have reported an old man with two young women in a black sedan coming from the cottage. If we stay together, we'll be spotted. Mingle with the crowd, dance in the street, and make your way separately to the chapel. We'll meet inside. My friend Arzhel will be wearing a blue sweater and a black beret, sitting in the front left pew." Jacques stepped back from Lola and Yvette and wandered away, meandering through the lively crowd.

"See you inside the chapel." Although Lola smiled,

worry clouded her bright brown gaze as she joined the procession heading toward the stone church with slanted grey slate roof.

Yvette strode among the jubilant villagers, observing the appetizing array of steaming seafood and delicious *crêpes* atop tables strewn with blue and white *faïence* porcelain. Black and white Breton flags, proudly displaying the ermine emblem of Brittany, flapped in the salty wind, overwhelmed by the ominous red banners bearing the black swastikas of the Third Reich.

As she merged with the parade making its way toward the chapel, Yvette froze as German soldiers swarmed the celebration, demanding identification papers from young women in the throng.

They're looking for me. And they know my name, thanks to Marie-Claire Dubois. Yvette's pulse hammered in her throat as two glowering Nazis headed straight for her.

She frantically searched for an escape, but armed German guards patrolled both sides of the street. If she tried to run, they'd seize her.

Or shoot her.

The thunderous thud of stomping black boots pounded in her ears.

I can't let them take me. I must get into the chapel!

Panicked, Yvette met the sympathetic gaze of a middle-aged woman standing behind her in the parade. *Maybe she'll help me. I have no other choice.*

"Please—the Germans are after me. I'm pregnant. They'll torture me… My baby and I will both die. Please help me get into the chapel." Yvette desperately clung to the woman's hand like a life preserver in a drowning, tumultuous sea.

"Of course. Lean on me. I'll say that you're ill and need to get out of the hot sun." The dark-haired stranger cradled Yvette's head against her ample bosom, wrapping a supportive arm around her shoulder as they pushed forward with the crowd.

Her legs shook violently as the Nazis stormed forward, a dizzying wave of nausea and terror liquefying her bowels. She buried her face in the woman's shoulder, suppressing the impossible urge to scream.

Yvette felt her arm tugged as the kind stranger led her away from imminent danger.

But the strident, traitorous shriek stabbed her straight through the heart. "*Here she is! The woman you want*!"

Each of two German guards angrily seized one of Yvette's trembling arms as she gaped in disbelief at the glaring, maniacal woman who had just betrayed her.

"She's the one you're hunting! She begged me to help her. As if I would risk my life for an enemy of the German army. *Heil Hitler*!" Rabid fanaticism blazed in the woman's crazed eyes as spittle flew from her puckered, perfidious lips.

Two additional SS Officers, their pistols drawn and aimed at Yvette, joined the pair of German soldiers restraining her. Yvette's satchel of herbs and shoulder bag fell from her shaking shoulders onto the crowded, cobblestone street.

Across the now-silent, stunned crowd, Yvette made desperate eye contact with Lola and Jacques.

Despair distorted their beloved faces. They watched in hopeless, helpless horror as the four armed, implacable SS officers roughly hauled Yvette away.

Chapter 12

Retribution

The four Nazis dragged her to a black sedan, similar to the one Jacques had stolen, and shoved her into the back seat. An armed SS Officer climbed in on either side to hem her in, barking in rapid German, which Yvette could not understand. The two other Nazis piled into the front seat, and as the driver sped away, the German officer beside him used a handheld radio to apparently call in a report. The only comprehensible word that Yvette could discern was the name Cancale.

They are taking me to their headquarters in Cancale. To the officer who met with Étienne Boucher. The Nazi who gunned down Papa, Jeffroi, and Jean-Michel.

The brutal beast who haunted her worst nightmares.

Yvette's hands were ice cold, her arms numb and tingling with shock, as the car careened along the craggy coast. When the driver turned onto the long, narrow dirt road leading to the familiar farmhouse perched on the peninsular point, she peered out the windows, mouth agape.

Her beloved family home had been transformed into a massive military garrison for formidable, frightening weapons of war.

In front of the neatly manicured rows of wooden buildings serving as barracks, hundreds of German soldiers practiced combat drills amid enormous tanks, artillery, armored vehicles, and cannons.

Preparing for battle.

The Battle of Saint-Malo.

Against the Allies and the Free French Forces. Including Beau, Jules, and les Loups.

A violent shiver slithered up Yvette's frozen spine.

While the black sedan barreled up the narrow dirt road toward the three-story white farmhouse on the cliff, Yvette stared at the heathered meadows on the outskirts of the property, where a herd of recently shorn sheep grazed peacefully, oblivious to the human machinations of war. Forced laborers toiled in the fields under the setting sun, tending crops to feed the voracious Wehrmacht army. On the opposite side of the farmhouse, to the east, charred rubble was all that remained of what must have once been additional rows of lodging to house the Nazi soldiers.

The French Resistance—with Jules and les Loups— must have blown up the barracks on that side. I wish they had destroyed it all.

Memories of childhood flooded Yvette as the black sedan parked in front of her former family home.

Harvesting shellfish in the sheltered cove with *Mamie* and Yanna. Planting crops and shearing sheep with Papa, Jeffroi, and Jean-Michel. Combing, carding, and spinning wool with *Maman* and *Mamie*. Racing across the heathered moor, playing *cache-cache*—hide and seek—with her three older brothers. Climbing the tallest trees with Jules, while *Maman* hollered at them to come down so they wouldn't break their necks.

Sadness and sorrow suffocated her.

Jules was the only one left of her entire family. The Nazis were bringing her here to be tortured. To force her into betraying her beloved brother. They'd use her to trap Jules. And all of them would die.

Unless… A mad, wild idea began to form in Yvette's analytical mind.

The Nazi soldier on her right exited the vehicle, grabbed Yvette's arm, and yanked her out the door. Although she stumbled, she avoided falling when one of the other German guards raced around the side of the car and seized her other arm. Together, they dragged her up the stone steps to the wooden entrance door, where two German soldiers stood guard. After a brief exchange in German, the driver of the car and the radio operator got back into the sedan and drove away, while Yvette's two armed guards hauled her into the house.

Inside the foyer, Yvette glimpsed the wooden stairs leading to the upper level bedrooms where she and her family had slept. To the left, the large, open living room with the huge stone fireplace and carved mantle that she, *Maman*, and *Mamie* had decorated every December with boughs of evergreen, holly, and hellebore from the nearby woods. The delicious aromas of *le Réveillon,* the Christmas Eve feast—complete with turkey stuffed with chestnuts and *Mamie*'s incredible *bûche de Noël,* the traditional chocolate Yulelog cake—came wafting to Yvette on the wind of fond remembrances of times gone by.

As she stood, overwhelmed with childhood memories and visions of family celebrations, the door to her father's former study opened at the end of the long hall.

A towering brute emerged in the doorway.

The same dark blond hair. Squat, bulbous nose and clefted, clenched chin.

The murderous monster who haunted her dreams.

"At last we meet, Yvette Fleury." A predatory smile spread across his square, savage jaw. He barked in German to the two guards, who dragged Yvette down the hall and into the room where the last rays of sunset streaked the summer sky and sea with vivid shades of violet, indigo, and mauve.

They shoved her into a wooden chair and retreated to stand guard just outside the door.

The glowering Nazi stood at military attention between the two open windows framing the lavender painted sky. His severe, steely gaze glinted with malice and unspeakable cruelty. *"I am Obersturmführer* Heinrich Balsch, Senior Storm Leader in the *Waffen-SS."*

With a snide smirk, he lowered himself into the chair across the table from her. "And you are the sister of Jules Antoine Fleury, leader of the French Resistance *maquis* hiding in the Breton woods.*"

Balsch leaned back in his chair and methodically crossed his brawny arms over the greyish green tunic of his impeccable Nazi uniform. "Section Leader Étienne Boucher recently came here to requisition Soviet soldiers—Russian Wolfhounds, he called them—to aid in his hunt for the radical Resistance group named *les Loups."* The SS Officer ran the tips of his long fingers over a neat stack of papers in a folder laid before him on the polished mahogany table. "Boucher also requested records from the *Carlingue* headquarters in Paris with the names of the French family who formerly inhabited this farmhouse."

Triumphant mockery laced his venomous voice, slithering up Yvette's spine. "How ironic that the men I sent to investigate Boucher's gruesome murder discovered a suspect named Yvette Fleury. The very same name which arrived from Gestapo headquarters for the family who once lived in this farmhouse. The foolish Frenchman and his three sons who refused to relinquish this residence and were gunned down by my men." Sadistic pleasure glinted in his smug smile. "Providing us with the name of the one son who miraculously survived the shooting and escaped into the nearby woods. *Jules Antoine Fleury.* Your brother."

A wicked gleam in his greedy eyes, Balsch leaned menacingly across the table, exalting in predatory power over his doomed prisoner. "You are the key, Yvette Fleury. The means for me to finally trap the alpha wolf *Garou* and his elusive pack, *les Loups.* The Resistance rebels that Section Leader Boucher hunted for four long years."

Resolute and unwavering, he clenched his chiseled jaw and hissed like a serpent ready to strike. "You will tell me who they are. Where they hide. Their plans. Their numbers. Which ports the Allies will attack. Where the reinforcements and supplies are dropped."

He licked his lips in wicked anticipation with a long, serpentine tongue. "My torturer knows how to inflict intolerable pain without life-threatening injury. Prolonging the exquisite agony for days—even weeks—before you finally succumb."

Lust flared as his lascivious gaze raked lewdly across Yvette's body and lingered on her full breasts. "But first, before I turn you over to him…you'll relieve the unbearable ache in my overflowing loins. It has been far too long since I've emptied them into a woman."

The *Obersturmführer* rose from his chair and called to one of his men standing in the hall.

A German soldier appeared in the doorway and saluted his commanding SS officer.

"It's going to be a long night," Balsch snickered in French so that Yvette would understand. "Make a pot of coffee." He spoke German to his attendant and grinned at Yvette as the deferential soldier disappeared down the hall. Balsch walked around the table, crossed the room, and closed the door.

Yvette, alone with the Nazi beast, stared at the back of his brutal skull, her daring idea rapidly taking shape.

In the breadth of a split second, her attention darted through the open window to the cliff at the edge of the sea where twilight cast shadows from the nearby woods. As children, she and Jules had discovered a narrow footpath which led from the forested ledge at the top of the bluff to the sandy beach a hundred feet below.

Where a hidden sea cave had provided countless adventures of marauding pirates and priceless buried treasure.

The German army thinks women are weak. Worthless except for alleviating male lust and breeding.

No one had examined Yvette for weapons. And Balsch was confident that she cowered in his commanding, controlling presence.

Without hesitation, Yvette retrieved the pistol from inside her bra. Unlatched the safety. And, in a frenzied flash, fired a silent shot directly into the base of the monster's malevolent skull.

Retribution.

For Papa, Jeffroi, and Jean-Michel.

For Jules, Beau, and les Loups.
For my baby. For me.
And for France.

She tucked the pistol back into her bra and quickly climbed through the open window, grateful that the barracks on the east side of the farmhouse had been destroyed. Sprinting across the heathered meadow, she ducked over the edge of the cliff, clambered down the narrow path, and landed on the sandy shore at the bottom of the bluff. Racing up the beach, she recognized the jut in the craggy shoreline which hid the mouth of the secret cave.

Although it was nearly dark, enough twilight remained for her to spot the entrance and slip into the grotto. She followed the curve of the tunnel, relying as much on memory as on the feel of the cave wall against her right hand. Her curved left arm formed a protective shield over her head as she advanced cautiously into the gloom.

Twenty minutes later, she emerged from the cave in the forest near the farmhouse of her neighbor, Mathieu Plou. In the light of the waxing moon, she spotted a bicycle leaning against the side of the wooden building.

I promise, if I survive, I will return or replace this means of escape.

Yvette had grown up in this neighborhood. She knew the area like the back of her hand. Climbing onto the bicycle and avoiding the main roads where the German vehicles would soon be searching for her, Yvette rode off into the dense Breton woods.

And headed west for Saint-Malo.

Chapter 13

The Medieval Fortress of Saint-Malo

Zach's leg was killing him. They'd been trudging through the forest for eight days, encountering sporadic enemy fire as they made their way slowly toward Saint-Malo. The constant marching, running, fighting, and sleeping on the ground had been brutal on his barely healed fracture where a constant ache now throbbed relentlessly. Traveling with a combined group of FFI French Resistance forces—including Jules and *les Loups*—and half a dozen US infantrymen, along with Murph and Mac, he was immensely relieved when they finally arrived at the outskirts of the fortified seaport of Saint-Malo.

They were greeted by Staff Sergeant Paul Driscoll, who led them inside a former hotel on the beach which now served as US army headquarters, command center, barracks, and hospital in Saint-Malo. Inside the crowded building, several officers consulted maps and discussed battle strategy around a large table while dozens of other soldiers relayed messages, radioed for updates, and hauled in boxes of medical supplies, rations, and equipment.

Driscoll led Zach, Jules, and their group of eighteen *Loups* and American soldiers through the commotion toward a hallway at the back of the enormous room. "This building—the Hotel Franklin—is in the American controlled section outside the walled inner city, where the Germans have several well-fortified garrisons. Saint-Malo used to be a medieval fortress, with a castle, keep, and ramparts to fend off attacks. The Germans fortified it with twenty-foot thick walls of steel and concrete, a system of underground bunkers, pillboxes, machine gunners, and telephone controls to the nearby channel islands where they've got coastal guns—transforming it into an impenetrable fortress. Shit, Allied planes have been bombing all week, with no effect. The whole city's on fire, but the German commander von Aulock—they call him the Mad Colonel—won't let the civilians put out the flames."

He led them from the large, open area bustling with activity, down a hall, and up a flight of wooden stairs. Along each side of the lengthy corridor, doors led to rooms of the former hotel. "We have barracks on this floor and the one above us. Most of the ground floor has been converted into a hospital. You can settle in, have a shower, catch some sleep." He opened the door to a small room with a single bed, wooden table, and chair. "Officers have private rooms, and this one's yours, Lieutenant Zachford. The rest are double accommodations for your men—two per room. I'll leave you here. The mess hall is downstairs, and chow is served at eighteen hundred hours. See you then, sir." Driscoll saluted Zach, nodded goodbye to the rest of the men, and headed back down the hall.

As the *Loups* divided into pairs, dispersing into their assigned rooms for much-needed sleep, Jules approached Zach with Briac, Gwilherm, and Pierrick.

"Our reports indicate that twenty thousand American infantrymen are here in Saint-Malo. They've taken Paramé, Saint-Ideuc, and Fort de la Varde—all the surrounding areas outside the city walls. Despite constant bombardment, the German forts have held, with little or no damage. In order to reach the citadel, where von Aulock and 600 Germans are encamped underground, they'll have to cross a 1000-yard-long exposed causeway. General Middleton is coordinating a bombardment to provide smokescreen for the American infantry to race across. A group of Resistance fighters are joining them. You can count on us to fight at your side." He gripped Zach's arm, fraternal respect glowing in his lupine gaze. "Get some sleep. We'll talk later. At chow."

As Jules and *les Loups* sauntered down the hall, Zach entered his room, dropped his backpack on the floor, and stripped off his filthy uniform, boots, and helmet. Debilitating pain pulsated in his left leg, and he was eager to get his weight off of it. He was profoundly grateful that his private quarters included a bathroom with running water, an amenity he'd not enjoyed since his arrival in France. Standing under the hot shower, he moaned with pleasure as he washed away the layers of grime and sweat, soothing the pain in his badly swollen limb.

Exulting in the sensual delight of clean hair and skin, Zach took the razor from his combat pack and shaved away a week's worth of stubble. With a sigh of contentment, he crawled into bed and slept like a log.

Slanted rays of the sun setting over the western Atlantic Ocean streamed in through the window of his room as Zach awoke and checked the watch on his bedside table. *Chow's in fifteen minutes. Time to get up.*

He retrieved a clean uniform and socks from his gear, got dressed, and met Mac, Murph, Jules, and *les Loups* in the hall when he exited his room. Together, they went downstairs to the mess hall where they would receive orders for the planned siege of the citadel.

Zach joined the rest of the soldiers waiting in line to receive a ration of goulash—hot stew made from sausage with potatoes and vegetables—a hunk of bread, a wedge of cheese, and a cup of coffee. *I haven't had real coffee in months. Damn, it smells good.* He sat at the table with Jules and his men, profoundly grateful for the first hot meal since he'd left *le Vivier-Sur-Mer.*

While the men ate, Colonel Brett Lipscomb from the 83rd Infantry addressed the group. "The Germans have destroyed the harbor, docks, and quays, to prevent us from using it to reinforce our ranks. The German commander, von Aulock, evacuated all French civilians from a ten-mile designated combat zone—roughly the range of the coastal guns on the island of *Cézembre*—but a lot have stayed behind to help us fight. The Nazis set the city on fire, but we plan to use that smokescreen to our advantage."

He referred to a large map displayed on the wall. "The Germans have several well-stocked garrisons within the ramparts of the old city. They transformed a quarry into a fortification with tunnels and bunkers. Six feet below ground, protected by twenty foot thick walls of steel and concrete. We'll have to apply siege warfare tactics to break through their defenses." Lipscomb pointed to a diagram of the inner city. "Our men will scale the walls of the medieval castle to get inside the courtyard. And drop pole charges down the ventilator shafts. We're coordinating bombardments to provide cover. The siege is set for Friday at 0600 hours. You'll receive further orders tomorrow."

As the colonel returned to the table to join the high ranking officers and enjoy his meal, a corporal rushed through the entrance door and stopped to speak to Staff Sergeant Paul Driscoll, the soldier who had escorted Zach and his men to their quarters. Driscoll arose from his table and led the corporal to Jules. "Jules Fleury? Two civilians have just arrived, requesting to speak to you with an urgent message."

Jules shot a surprised glance at Zach, then replied to the corporal. "Please, bring them in."

Zach's jaw dropped open at the sight of Lola and Jacques Blanchard. *What are they doing here? And where's Yvette?* He sprang to his feet, his pulse racing at the sudden surge of panic.

Jules took Lola's hands, his brows furrowed in apprehension. "Why are you here? What's happened?"

Lola collapsed into Jules' arms and choked out a sob. "The Nazis took Yvette."

Zach struggled to breathe.

Cradling Lola against his chest, a desperate Jules fixed his gaze on Jacques Blanchard. "Where?"

"To Cancale. To your old farmhouse." Jacques gratefully accepted a glass of water from Briac and gulped down a few swallows. He lowered himself onto a chair beside Gwilherm and Pierrick, who had huddled around to listen. "The SS Officer in command there sent four men into the village to investigate the Butcher's death. I overheard them asking questions about Yvette. They were arresting her for interrogation."

A sickening wave of horror flooded Zach.

They'll torture her.
And kill her.

Jules seated Lola and pulled up a chair beside her, leaning over to clutch both her hands.

Zach collapsed onto a chair, his limbs shaking, his stomach twitching, as Jacques continued. "I sped home, grabbed the MP 40 you'd given me. Lola had the key to the back door of Yvette's cottage, so I snuck in through the kitchen. And gunned the bastards down in the living room."

Lola leaned toward Zach, her face crumpled with fear. "Yvette was hiding in the cellar. I knocked on the panel to let her know it was safe to come up. *Papi* and I dragged the bodies into the woods while she cleaned up the blood on the floor. We stole the German car and headed to Cherrueix. But we were spotted on the way. By another Nazi vehicle headed to the cottage."

"The SS men must have called in the report that they'd seen us, because German soldiers were everywhere in Cherrueix. They swarmed the parade, checking identification papers of all young women. They arrested Yvette and hauled her off. Lola and I met my friend Arzhel in the chapel as planned, and he drove us here." An overwrought Jacques rubbed his hands along his thighs, rocking back and forth in his chair. "How can we save Yvette?"

Jules—the alpha wolf *Garou*—commanded his pack. "We go back to Cancale. Briac, you and *les Loups* will lay explosives on the west side of the garrison. Take out the tanks and artillery to create a diversion. When the Germans come running out of the barracks, gun them down." He spun to Zach. "There's a cave in the woods that empties on the beach at the base of the cliff just below the farmhouse. You and I will take a group and infiltrate from the east. When Briac detonates the explosions, the Nazis will file out of the house to investigate, while we slip in and get Yvette." His lupine gaze blazed with fraternity and ferocity. "I grew up in that house. I know every room and passageway. We'll find her, Zach. *We will.*"

Zach stood, shook out his limbs, and rolled his head on his shoulders. "I need to speak with Captain Lipscomb. See if he can spare us a few men. Wait here."

The American officer listened attentively to Zach's account of a civilian hostage and the German troops, tanks, and artillery in Cancale which would undoubtedly arrive soon to reinforce the Nazi position in Saint-Malo. He assigned twenty men to assist in the rescue attempt. "Free the hostage, if possible." *If she's still alive.* Zach understood the unspoken message in Captain Lipscomb's words. "Take out the whole fucking garrison. Then report back here for the siege."

Zach, as a ranking First Lieutenant, would lead the men—including Murph, Mac, and the twenty US soldiers, along with Jules and the band of eighteen Loups—back to Cancale.

To take out the Nazi garrison on the peninsular cliff.

And save the woman he loved.

****

Alerted by the deep rumbling of engines, Yvette veered off the narrow road to hide in the woods, watching in the moonlight as two German trucks loaded with soldiers passed by. Although she'd had to make three such stops to avoid Nazi vehicles, if her luck held, she'd soon reach the outskirts of Saint-Malo.

And be reunited with Beau.

Lieutenant Richard Zachford of the 82nd Airborne. The man she loved with all her heart.

Exhausted, nauseous, and thirsty, Yvette rolled into the slumbering coastal town as it slowly awakened in the quiet, early morning light. Spotting an open café, she dismounted from her bicycle, leaned it up against the wall near the entrance door, and entered the bistro. The appetizing aroma of fresh coffee wafted into the briny air.

"Bonjour, Monsieur. Un croissant et un café, s'il vous plaît." Yvette sat on a barstool at the counter and placed her order. Glancing around at the various tables in the small restaurant, she spotted a few local fishermen and several American soldiers eating breakfast. When the proprietor returned with her croissant and coffee, she asked him how she might reach American headquarters to volunteer as a nurse and inquire about finding missing friends and family.

He wiped off the countertop as Yvette devoured her meager meal. "The Americans have transformed a hotel into US headquarters—with a command center, lodging for soldiers and volunteers, and a hospital—right here on the beach." He gave her the name and address of the Franklin Hotel. "They're desperate for nurses. The Nazis have cannons and artillery on an island three miles offshore, and they've repelled every American attempt to break through the inner city walls. There's a lot of wounded soldiers, and the hospital needs all the medical help they can get. They might even be able to help you find your family. *Bonne chance, Mademoiselle.* I wish you the best of luck. "

Yvette thanked the owner, paid her bill with the few coins she'd tucked inside her pocket back at the cottage, and left the café. She climbed back on her bicycle, exhaled forcefully, and headed west toward the beach.

The Hotel Franklin was an enormous four-story building facing the Atlantic Ocean, accessible to vehicles by its location on a wide, paved street. As Yvette rode her bike toward the hotel, a military ambulance displaying a large red cross raced up to the entrance. American soldiers quickly unloaded four stretchers from the back, as hospital personnel rushed outside to bring the wounded victims in for medical treatment. Jeeps arrived, soldiers filed in and out of the building, with civilians bringing medical supplies and equipment to aid military medics in treating the wounded.

Yvette leaned her stolen bicycle against the outer wall and went inside, where she glimpsed a receptionist area amid the hectic activity of bustling medical personnel and American soldiers.

She was greeted by a blonde woman in a green Army uniform adorned with gold insignia, including a medical symbol and a circular patch which read *Army Nurse Corps*. "Hello, I'm Lieutenant Marjorie Novak. May I help you?"

Yvette smiled weakly, relieved to have made it to American headquarters. Her English was not excellent, but she spoke adequately enough to understand the woman and respond to her question. "My name is Yvette Fleury. I am a healer, and I have come to volunteer as a nurse. But I'm also trying to find Lieutenant Richard Zachford of the 82nd Airborne, 507th Parachute Infantry Regiment. And my brother, Jules Fleury, a member of the Free French Forces from *le Vivier-Sur-Mer*. Do you know how I might reach either of them?"

Lieutenant Novak consulted the files on her desk

and shook her head. "Neither name is listed here, but I'll take yours—and theirs—to keep in our records. The International Relief and Rescue Committee is working to reunite displaced families and help them find missing or wounded soldiers. So is the International Red Cross. Perhaps one of these organizations might help you locate them." The army nurse recorded Yvette's information on the paper attached to her clipboard. "In the meantime, I'll take you to meet the coordinator of our volunteer nurses, Lieutenant Mary Blake. She'll provide you with lodging, uniforms, shoes…and explain about mealtimes and duties. We are desperate for nurses and medical assistants and are truly grateful for every volunteer. Thank you very much for offering your service, Mademoiselle Fleury. Please, follow me."

Yvette accompanied the receptionist down a long corridor to a nurses' station where several women dressed in US army uniforms of crisp green blouses, skirts, and caps were unpacking boxes of medical supplies, recording information as they stored the provisions, conferring as they checked charts. "This is the nurses' station where supplies and records are kept. I'll introduce you to Lieutenant Blake. She's in charge of our civilian volunteers."

At Lieutenant Novak's gesture, a tall, thin nurse with chin-length, wavy brown hair approached with a friendly smile to greet them.

"Mary, this is Yvette Fleury, a new civilian volunteer. Please introduce her to the others and help her get settled." Lieutenant Novak nodded goodbye to Yvette. "I'll leave you in Lieutenant Blake's capable hands. She speaks fluent French, so you'll have no trouble communicating. Thank you again for volunteering, Mademoiselle Fleury. Good luck in finding your loved ones." The competent military nurse shook Yvette's hand and strode briskly down the hall, back to her busy reception desk.

"Well, as I'm sure Lieutenant Novak already told you, we're desperate for nurses and grateful for every single volunteer." The cheerful nurse spoke French to Yvette, then switched to English as she informed her colleagues that she'd return after welcoming her new recruit. Mary Blake's kind features exuded warmth as she led Yvette down the hospital corridor, past quiet rooms with closed doors. "Our civilian volunteers fetch supplies for doctors or nurses, run errands, serve meals to the patients who can eat. They empty bedpans...sponge bathe the wounded soldiers. Sit with them. Talk to them. Keep them company. It's therapeutic for the injured to know that we care about them. Sometimes, it even gives them the will to live." Compassionate strength shone in her expressive, intelligent eyes.

At the end of the hall, they arrived at a vast, open room where nurses tended wounded soldiers in neat, orderly rows of white hospital beds. A wave of nausea washed over Yvette at the astringent odor of antiseptics and bleach mingling with the coppery stench of blood, sickness, and gore.

Inside the enormous hospital area, injured patients were covered in bandages, many with broken legs in suspended plaster casts. Some were hooked up to IV drips, rubber tubes, or machines. Beside a few hospital beds, women in white caps and white aprons bearing a red cross held hands, read books, or sponged the brows of battered, bloodied soldiers.

Lieutenant Blake fetched a parcel from a cupboard on the wall and handed it to Yvette. "Inside, you'll find a white cap and apron, like the ones you see on our volunteers in this room. We have rotating shifts with breaks for meals, so you'll be well-fed and get plenty of rest. We also provide accommodations for hospital volunteers on the top three floors of this building. I'll assign you a room and take you up so you can shower and rest. You look exhausted. Did you just arrive?"

Yvette smiled weakly and nodded. "Yes, I did. Yesterday, I escaped the Nazi garrison in Cancale. I rode a bicycle all night long, keeping to the woods to avoid the Germans. I just arrived here about an hour ago. I haven't slept at all."

"Well, let me find you a room right now so we can remedy that." Lieutenant Blake retrieved a folder from a filing cabinet against the wall. "Did you say you're from Cancale?"

Childhood memories of the beloved family farmhouse flooded Yvette, quickly displaced by haunting images of *Obersturmführer* Balsch, SS Officers, and Nazi monsters with machine guns. She shuddered violently and replied, "I rode from Cancale, but I live in *le Vivier-Sur-Mer.*"

The army nurse's brows lifted in surprise. "*Le Vivier-Sur-Mer*? We have another civilian volunteer from that village. Let me check…" She perused a list from her folder. "Ah, yes. Here it is. Lola Blanchard. She and her grandfather Jacques arrived yesterday. She's in room 322, and he is right next door, in 323. I can place you with her, if you like?"

Yvette swooned with relief, her eyes brimming with tears. "Yes, that would be wonderful. Thank you very much. She and I are close friends."

"Perfect. Here's your key. I'll bring you up to the room right now." Lieutenant Driscoll handed Yvette a hotel key to room 322. "Come, the stairwell is just beyond this exit door."

Clutching the bag which held her volunteer nurse's uniform against her chest, Yvette followed the civilian coordinator from the hospital room, up the stairs, and down the hall to room 322.

Lieutenant Mary Blake knocked on the door and smiled at Yvette, her cheerful expression bright with hope.

When the door opened, Yvette nearly collapsed at the welcome sight of Lola's soft brown curls and astounded, beloved face.

"Yvette! Thank God!" Lola threw her arms around Yvette, pulling her close, rocking back and forth as she sobbed with joy. After a moment, she stepped aside to welcome Yvette into the room. "Please, come in. How did you escape?"

Lieutenant Blake addressed Lola from the doorway. "Miss Fleury just arrived this morning to volunteer as a nurse. I've placed her as your roommate, since you're friends. I'll leave her with you now. Please bring her downstairs for lunch, show her around. Check in with me tomorrow morning at the nurses' station. Until then, thank you both again very much for volunteering at our hospital. See you soon." With a pleasant smile and a cordial wave goodbye, the nurse coordinator returned to her duties.

Lola hugged Yvette again and led her into a beige room where soft white curtains framed a sunny window overlooking the sea. On each of the opposing walls, a wooden dresser stood beside a single bed with a navy blue comforter and a lamp atop a small nightstand. Under the window, between the two twin beds, a teapot sat on a hotplate atop a wooden table where two tufted chairs offered practical, comfortable seating.

And, on top of the nightstand near the untouched bed, Yvette spotted her satchel of herbs and the shoulder bag that she'd dropped during her arrest at Cherrueix. "My supplies!"

"After the Nazis left, I sauntered back over to fetch them." Lola's chin quivered as her big brown eyes brimmed with tears. She hugged Yvette and stammered, "I wanted to keep them—because they were yours."

"Thank you very much, Lola. I'm grateful to have my herbs. And a change of clothes, too." Her legs wobbly from the long bike ride and shaking from the traumatic ordeal, Yvette plopped into a chair and exhaled in relief. She looked imploringly at Lola. "There's no record of Beau or Jules. Have you heard anything since you've been here?"

The anguish that crossed Lola's face was answer enough. "Wait here while I get *Papi*. I'll be right back." She slipped out the door and into the hall.

Trying to dispel an overwhelming surge of panic and debilitating nausea, Yvette inhaled deeply to settle her shattered nerves. *She needs Jacques to tell me the bad news. Please, let it not be Beau or Jules...* Her breathing shallow and ragged, Yvette's pulse raced and her mouth went dry.

Jacques' kind, crinkled visage appeared in the doorway. "Yvette, thank God you're here!"

She rose unsteadily from the chair, gripping the edge of the table to brace for the impact of the information that

Lola was reluctant to share.

Jacques hugged Yvette tight, shuddering with silent sobs. After a few moments, he sat her down on the edge of the bed and pulled up a chair to perch beside her. "How did you escape?"

Lola lifted the teapot from the hotplate and poured a cup, handing it to Yvette.

She accepted it gratefully, taking a few sips to compose herself and slake her raging thirst. "The Nazis took me out to the farmhouse on the cliff. The family home where I used to live. Where I saw them gun down my father and brothers." Yvette choked on a sob, swallowing her sorrow with more gulps of tea. "I met the commanding officer who gave the order…" Her voice cracked as Lola sat down on the bed beside her and squeezed her trembling hand. Empathy radiated from Lola's expression, blurred by the tears which Yvette blinked away. "I killed him." She spat out the hatred and fury blazing in her bitter soul. "With the pistol Jules gave me." Yvette stared into the dark depths of Jacques' shrewd, knowing gaze. "I snuck up behind him. And shot the bastard in the back of the head."

She spun toward a stunned, shocked Lola. "I escaped through an open window. Sprinted across the grass to the top of the cliff, down a path to the beach far below. When Jules and I were children, we discovered a hidden sea cave there that leads into the forest. That's how I got away. I followed the cave tunnel under the cliff. Emerged in the woods near a neighbor's farm. Stole a bike. And rode all night to Saint-Malo."

Lola, sitting beside Yvette on the bed, pulled her into a fierce, desperate hug. "I'm so glad you escaped."

Yvette held her dear friend, then extricated herself

from the tight embrace. "Now, please tell me. Have you found Beau and Jules?"

Lola glanced at her grandfather, despair dimming her bright gaze.

"They've gone to Cancale. *To rescue you.*" Jacques' deep voice tolled like a heavy bourdon bell.

Ironic horror descended like doom.

Gut clenching, throat constricting, Yvette buried her face in her hands.

And howled like a wounded wolf.

Chapter 14

A Former Pitcher

Hidden among the oak, beech, and pine trees, Zach huddled with Jules, Briac, Gwilherm, and Pierrick at the forested edge to the west of the open meadow near the farmhouse. Moonlight illuminated the five rows of rectangular wooden buildings that served as barracks for the military garrison at Cancale.

"It's all gone. The tanks, trucks, artillery, equipment. Everything that was here before." Jules eyed the empty field beyond the woods where they now stood among the thick trees.

"No lights on in the farmhouse. No guards on patrol. Nothing. It looks deserted." Wariness blazed in Briac's assessing scowl. "I'll send scouts to check out the barracks." He stole away from Zach to confer with several *Loups* from his pack.

Swiftly and silently, four men slipped across the meadow toward the wooden encampment while the rest of the regiment aimed weapons to provide cover if necessary. After a few minutes, the scouts returned to report that the buildings were indeed empty.

"Lay the explosives under the barracks and watch for my signal. Zach and I will take our group through the woods and infiltrate the farmhouse from the east. I'll signal with the flashlight. One flash—the house is empty. Two flashes—detonate, to create the diversion." Jules left orders for *les Loups* with Briac, Pierrick, and Gwilherm. With a swoop of his arm, he led Zach, Mac, Murph, and a combined group of *Loups* and American soldiers into the dense woods. "We won't need to use the cave on the beach and scale the cliff, since there are no patrols anywhere on the grounds. We'll just hide behind the rubble of the old barracks on this side. And slip into the house from there."

The crashing of waves against the cliff far below the farmhouse was the only sound in the velvety stillness of the night. Stars winked in the black sky where moonlight filtered through scattered clouds blown by the brisk, salty breeze.

"That window leads into my father's study. From there, the hall leads to the stairwell." Jules gave orders, assigning men to search each level, then dashed across the meadow to the opened window of the farmhouse. He slid over the sill, climbing inside the study, and motioned for the first group to follow.

Zach and six of his men sprinted across the field while the rest remained behind to provide cover. He climbed through the open window to join Jules in a spacious room where an oval mahogany table and six tufted wood chairs were slightly askew, pushed to one side. As the rest of the men entered the study and filtered down the hall, weapons drawn, the next group crossed the meadow and climbed through the window.

Jules directed them down the hall and up the stairs to search the top two levels while Zach and six men followed him through each room on the ground floor. It was obvious from the utter silence and profound darkness that the abandoned farmhouse was indeed deserted.

While Jules flashed one light to signal that the house was empty, Zach staggered down the hall toward the study as the stark horror descended upon him. *The Nazis wouldn't take a prisoner with them into battle. They killed Yvette here. Before they left.*

Moonlight shone through the open window onto a dark stain on the floor just inside the entrance at his feet. His mouth went dry, and his throat clenched as the grim reality sank in. *That's her blood. They killed her right here.*

Unable to breathe, the wind knocked out of him like violent blow to the gut, he dropped to his knees and buried his head in his hands.

I promised her that I would survive this bloody war. That I'd come back to marry her. We were going to spend the rest of our lives together. But they killed her. The Nazis murdered my beautiful Yvette.

Consumed with rage and inconsolable grief, Zach leapt to his feet and slammed his six foot four inch fury against the frame of the wooden door. Pummeling his pain through long, lanky arms, he pulverized the impenetrable wood, bellowing like a wounded beast. When his vehemence was at last spent, he collapsed into a senseless heap over the stain of Yvette's blood on the cold pinewood floor.

Jules slumped against a wall in the outer hall. Concealing his misery inside the crook of his bent arm, he keened in harrowing, agonizing anguish.

A few moments later, Jules wiped his face against the sleeve of his shirt. He extended a fraternal hand and helped Zach to his feet. Gripping Zach's twitching arm,

Jules' lupine gaze blazed feral and fierce in the dim moonlight. "C'mon. Let's blow up this fucking garrison. Go back to Saint-Malo. And annihilate the bloody bastards who killed Yvette."

Numb with shock, Zach stumbled down the hall and out the front door, blindly following Jules in a hazy, fog-like stupor. When they rejoined the combined regiment of American soldiers and FFI Resistance members at the edge of the woods, Briac blew up the barracks.

Zach watched the explosive flames unfurl into the black sky, bleak as his empty soul. *What do I have to live for without Yvette? It doesn't matter anymore if I survive this war. The fucking Nazis took her from me. I'll kill every one of them that I can. For her.*

In the cloud-scattered moonlight, the bone-weary company trudged west, back through the woods toward Saint-Malo, avoiding the main roads and potential enemy fire. Utterly exhausted, they'd already marched ten miles to Cancale, destroyed the remainder of the military barracks at the German garrison, and now needed to return for the planned siege of the medieval fortress. Fatigue was taking its heavy toll. It was essential to stop and get some sleep. They'd be in no condition to fight otherwise.

Zach spotted a dilapidated farmhouse and separate barn in a clearing up ahead. He sent four scouts to investigate and inspect. When they returned to report that both buildings were abandoned, he assigned guards to patrol the area in shifts while the men took turns catching a few hours of much-needed rest. Knowing he wouldn't be able to sleep himself, consumed with overwhelming sorrow, Zach volunteered for the first two-hour rotation.

Jules, Mac, and Murph insisted on joining him,

dispersing so that each man guarded a quarter of the perimeter of their extemporaneous camp.

As he sat down on a broken log to ease the throbbing in his bad leg, memories of Yvette flooded his senses. Silver eyes, haunted with horrors of the past. Wild mane of cascading black curls. Healing hands that soothed his wounds. Sensuous lips and body that stoked his passion. Shattered soul that had just begun to mend. Heroic heart, willing to sacrifice herself to the Butcher to save the ones she loved.

The woman he'd chosen to become his wife.

Murdered by the same monster who'd killed her father and brothers.

I'll track him down. And kill him with my bare hands.

Anguish, despair, and frustrated fury deafened Zach to the stealthy approach.

A flash of reflected moonlight caught his eye just as the first shots were fired.

Grabbing his MP 40, Zach unloaded a barrage of bullets into the thicket where the gunfire had originated. Four Soviet Cossack soldiers dropped to the ground.

Russian Wolfhounds. The ones the Butcher requisitioned to hunt down les Loups.

In a split second, all hell broke loose.

American soldiers simultaneously opened fire from the two windows on the upper level and the open doors on the ground floor of the barn while those inside the demolished farmhouse scrambled for cover behind the remains of stone walls and crumbling foundation. A dozen German soldiers pelted both buildings from behind a cluster of trees on Zach's left while the Soviets discharged machine guns from the sheltered grove on his right.

Caught in the crossfire between the company of Russian Wolfhounds and the group of Nazis, Jules and four American infantrymen were isolated and trapped in a small copse of trees.

I have to save Jules. Yvette desperately wanted her brother to live. I have to save him for her. And for Lola.

Even if I have to sacrifice myself.

In high school, Zach had been a standout pitcher for the Traip Academy baseball team. In college, at the University of Maine, he'd been damned proud of his ninety mph fastball, as well as the accuracy and control of his pitching arm. If he could just make it to the boulder about sixty yards ahead of where he now crouched in the woods, he could launch a volley of grenades into the thicket of trees and take out the cluster of Germans on the south side of the farmhouse. But in order to do so, he'd have to sprint across an open field—vulnerable to enemy fire—in full view of the Russian Wolfhounds on his right. And, although it was dark and well past midnight, the nearly full moon shone brightly onto the clearing near the rock.

Zach had run track in college—he'd always been a swift runner—but he would have nowhere near his former speed now, with his injured leg barely healed and throbbing like hell. Still, if he could reach the stone slab, he could shield himself from the Wolfhounds while hurling the grenades at the cluster of Germans.

Heart racing and muscles roaring from the sudden surge of adrenaline, Zach leapt from his hidden guard post and bolted toward the huge rock.

A barrage of gunfire pelted the leaf-strewn ground, striking the boulder as sparks and chunks of stone flew high into the air. As he ran, pumping his arms like pistons to gain momentum, a searing, burning pain shot up his left leg as two bullets entered his rear calf.

Fighting the blinding agony, Zach dropped to his knees, pulled the pin, and launched the first grenade into the cluster of trees where the Nazis had been firing upon him from the left. As the explosion sent a plume of flames high into the black sky, he threw another grenade into the thicket, profoundly grateful for his accurate pitching arm.

As a furious blaze consumed soldiers and trees, the piercing screams of dying men rent the ghastly night air. American snipers fired from the upper level of the barn and the interior of the farmhouse, eliminating the remainder of the Nazis and freeing Jules and the four trapped soldiers from the enemy threat on the left.

The burning in his calf was excruciating, and the pant leg of his uniform was saturated and dripping. Blood pooled into a large puddle on the ground near his left knee. He'd have to be quick—before he passed out. Summoning the last of his strength, he fired the remaining two grenades into the copse of trees where the Russian Wolfhounds were pelleting bullets from the right. Two more deafening explosions and a volley of rapid machine gun fire from the Americans in the barn silenced the Soviet menace as solemn stillness blanketed the smoke-filled air.

I'm woozy and light-headed from blood loss. Thank God—and my pitching arm—I saved Jules.

Zach collapsed headfirst into a gruesome heap of mud and blood.

****

The stench of rotten fish and slimy seaweed filled

his nostrils as Zach drifted in and out of consciousness. His lips were dry and cracked, his inflamed leg was on fire, and his whole body shook with violent chills. Jules and the rock-solid Pierrick supported him under the shoulders, dragging him through murky water along the forested edge of a foul-smelling swamp. The scorching summer sun beat mercilessly on his bare, drooped head, blinding him with reflected glare from the gloomy, brackish marsh.

"Water," he croaked through a constricted, parched throat.

Jules ordered his men to halt while he retrieved a canteen and poured water into Zach's desiccated mouth. "Hang in there, Zach. We're cutting through this marsh to avoid a platoon of Germans. We'll get you to a hospital. Stay with me, *mon frère*. We'll be there soon."

Chapter 15

A Forgotten Vial

The astringent odor of bleach and antiseptic was asphyxiating. A blinding overhead light prevented Zach from opening his eyes. Whirring, buzzing, and beeping blasted his sensitive ears, intensifying the mounting pressure inside his burgeoning skull. Inside his calf, a branding iron seared and savagely tore through flesh which throbbed and pulsed with relentless, debilitating pain.

Through the thick, suffocating haze of agony, Zach imagined Yvette's soft hand caressing his stubbled cheek. Her lilting voice soothed his torturous torment like a cool, cleansing cascade.

I must be dead. And in heaven. Because Yvette is here with me.

Zach succumbed to the welcome oblivion of darkness, overjoyed to be reunited with the woman he loved.

****

"I've given him a blood transfusion to replace what he lost. He's receiving intravenous fluids and morphine for the pain. But he's got a life-threatening bacterial infection in his left calf. If left untreated, gangrene will set in, and we'll have no choice but to amputate his leg.

He needs surgery to remove the two deeply embedded bullets, but without antibiotics, surgery is too risky because the infection will spread through his blood and kill him. If only I had some penicillin, I could save his life and possibly his leg. But our stores are exhausted, and there's none of the antibiotic left." Captain Joseph Ferguson, US Army Medical Doctor, informed Yvette in French of Zach's bleak prognosis as she caressed the side of his unconscious cheek and whispered in his unhearing ear. At the mention of the word *penicillin*, Yvette sprang up with a jolt.

"Penicillin?" The name jarred her memory.

She'd found a flask labeled penicillin in the cellar, the day she'd hidden from the SS men who had come to the cottage to arrest her. Not knowing what it was, thinking it must have fallen from Beau's backpack, she'd tucked it into her stash of medicinal herbs, intending to return it to him. She'd forgotten all about it until now. Pulse hammering in her throat, Yvette rasped, "I have a vial of penicillin in my room. I'll go get it right now."

Yvette zigzagged through the hospital beds where nurses tended their patients, dashing through the exit door and racing up the stairs to her room. Breathless, she fumbled with the key in the lock, threw open the door, and stumbled to the nightstand beside her bed. She snatched her satchel of herbs, flung it open, and fetched the metal vial from an interior leather pouch. Yvette verified the label, where the name *Penicillin* was clearly visible.

Clutching the precious flask to her breast, she dashed out into the hall, slammed the door shut behind her, and flew down the stairs, back to the large hospital room where Captain Ferguson and Lieutenant Mary

Blake hovered over a still-unconscious Beau.

Yvette wove quickly through the patients, desperate to deliver the medicine which might save Beau's life. Panting and shaking, she handed the vial to Dr. Ferguson, who scrutinized the label.

"Where did you get this vial?" The doctor turned the container over in his hand, closely examining the contents.

"From Lieutenant Zachford's backpack. I kept him hidden from the Nazis in my cellar, and it must have fallen out. When I found it, I didn't know what it was, but since it appeared to be medicine, I secured it in my satchel of healing herbs. I forgot all about it until you mentioned the name penicillin." She pointed to the vial in his hands. "Can you use it to save Beau—Lieutenant Zachford?"

"Indeed I can. This is exactly what I need to eradicate the bacterial infection." The military doctor conferred with nurse Blake, who returned a few moments later with alcohol, cotton balls, and a sterile syringe. She swabbed Beau's arm with alcohol while Doctor Ferguson extracted the proper dosage of penicillin from the vial into the hypodermic needle. He injected the antibiotic into Beau's bicep, then spoke to Yvette. "I'm going to wait twenty-four hours for the penicillin to take effect. We'll prep him tonight and perform the surgery tomorrow. I'll remove the bullets, repair the torn tissues and ligaments, and withdraw any splinters of shattered bone. If he survives the procedure, the penicillin will save his life. Hopefully, the surgery can save his leg as well."

Yvette leaned over Beau, whispering words of comfort and encouragement into his ear as Lola approached her side.

"I'll inform everyone of Zach's condition so you can stay here with him. Most of *les Loups* have returned to the FFI command post in a nearby building, and the American soldiers reported to US headquarters here. Jules is covered in swamp muck, so I'm taking him up to our room for a shower—and so he and I can be alone together for a little while. Tomorrow, he and the *Loups* will join the Allies in the siege on the citadel…" Lola's taut voice broke as she stoically blinked back tears.

Yvette hugged her tight and stroked the soft curls on the back of Lola's head. "Enjoy this precious time together. *Carpe diem.* Seize the day. Make every moment count. I'll be here when you come back down. Bring Jules with you—so I can hug him, too. Now, go. And lavish him with your love."

Brown eyes melting like milk chocolate, Lola squeezed Yvette's hand and dashed off to join Jules in the outer hall.

Lieutenant Mary Blake had arranged for volunteer nurses to care for Yvette's patients so that she could stay at Beau's side. Wiping his feverish brow, she traced her fingertips along his bristled cheek, murmuring words of love, hope, and strength into his unconscious ear. "You promised to survive, Beau. To come back and marry me. You must stay strong. Fight for your life. Come back to me, Beau. I love you. *Please live.*" She kissed his stubbled face and sat down in the chair at his bedside, holding his calloused hand and thumbing the tufts of hair at the base of his long, calloused fingers.

Please, God. Let him survive. So I can tell him about the baby. So he and I can get married. So we can become a family. Please don't take him from us. I pray you'll let him live.

The setting sun streamed in through the western windows facing the sea, gilding Beau with golden light like a divine benediction from above.

He's bathed in heavenly light. May it infuse him with the strength to survive.

A military nurse arrived, checked Beau's chart, and added another saline bag to his IV drip. She smiled reassuringly at Yvette. "Tonight, we'll prep him for surgery. First thing in the morning, we'll take him to the operating ward. If all goes well, after a period of postop observation, he'll be transferred to a recovery room, where you can join him." Encouragement exuded from her optimistic, enthusiastic voice. "Dr. Ferguson is an exemplary surgeon. Your soldier is in *very* capable hands." With another bright smile, the cheerful nurse ducked her chin and strode away to tend to her next patient.

Yvette gazed down at the man she loved. His noble visage was at peace, for the morphine eliminated his pain, but his mangled leg was horribly swollen, distended, and oozing noxious fluids. It didn't matter to her at all if he lost the limb, but she knew it would mean a great deal to Beau. Dr. Ferguson insisted on attempting surgery to save the leg, but Yvette just wanted him to survive. *At least with the penicillin, he has a chance. Please God, let him live. My baby needs a father. And I can't bear a life without Beau.*

As she sat, lost in her thoughts, Lola and Jules crossed the large hospital room to join her.

Yvette rose to her feet and flung her arms around her brother, rocking him back and forth. "Thank you for saving him. I am so profoundly grateful to have you and

Beau here. I love you, Jules. I was deathly afraid I'd lost you both."

Jules held her tight, cocooning her in a fraternal embrace. "I love you, too, *ma petite soeur.*" After a few moments, he released her and turned toward Lola. Deep voice rumbling with emotion, he pulled her against his chest. "I need to get back." He leaned down to softly brush her lips with his own. "I'm glad we had this time together. It'll give me strength when I need it most. *Je t'aime*, Lola. Always remember…I'm yours." Lupine eyes ablaze, Jules kissed Lola's hand, then each of Yvette's cheeks with *la bise* of farewell. With one last look of love and longing, he turned on his heels, strode across the vast room, and went out the hospital door.

An army nurse in a crisp green uniform came to check on Beau. She smiled softly at Yvette and Lola. "I need to take his vitals. Sponge bathe him and prep him for surgery. Why don't the two of you go get something to eat in the mess hall and come back in about an hour? I'll stay with him the whole time. I promise."

Lola took Yvette's hand and gave it a gentle tug. "C'mon. I'm starved. Lieutenant Sullivan will take good care of him." She grinned at the competent nurse examining Beau's chart. "Thank you very much. Be back in an hour."

****

Yvette dozed fitfully in the chair beside Beau's bed. He sputtered in his sleep a few times but never awakened. When morning came, Dr. Ferguson, Nurse Blake, and two orderlies came for him.

"We're taking him in for surgery now." A reassuring smile reached Dr. Ferguson's kind, compassionate gaze. "It will most likely be a few hours. Go get some coffee.

Maybe a bit of breakfast. There's a waiting area outside the operating ward. I'll come find you when it's over." He nodded goodbye, turned on his heels, and strode confidently down the corridor.

Yvette's mouth went dry, her stomach clenched, and her eyes filled with tears. *He's young and strong. And Dr. Ferguson is a fine surgeon. I must have faith. Beau will survive.*

Lola's steadfast presence comforted Yvette during the four long, torturous hours of surgery. When Dr. Ferguson finally appeared in the hall, his smile lit up Yvette's entire soul.

"He made it through the operation just fine. I removed the two bullets, surgically repaired the torn tissues and ligaments, and cut away a small section of gangrenous flesh. Fortunately, we caught it in time, and I did not need to amputate the leg. We'll keep him in the recovery room for a few hours until he's medically stable, then you can join him when he's transferred to the surgical ward." Dr. Ferguson shook Yvette's hand, then Lola's. With a professional smile and a courteous nod goodbye, he excused himself to return to surgery.

Yvette sank into her chair as tears of profound relief streamed down her cheeks. *Thank you, God, for answering my prayers. Beau is going to live!*

Lola, standing near her chair, cradled Yvette's head against her chest, bending down to kiss the wild, unkempt mane. "Did you hear that? Zach is going to be just fine!" She sat down beside Yvette, taking hold of her hands with an affectionate squeeze. Her unbridled spark of joy suddenly dimmed with worry and pain. "Now, we must pray for Jules, the *Loups*, and the American soldiers. Today, they charge the citadel."

****

Zach was groggy and disoriented. The antiseptic odor was strong, and his throat was parched and raw. Bandages covered his injured leg, and an IV tube was strapped to his left forearm. He struggled to open his eyes. And nearly jumped off the bed at the sight of a smiling, jubilant Yvette.

"*Bonjour, mon amour*. Welcome back." She rose to her feet and bent down to kiss his cheek. A soft tendril of her beautiful black curls caressed his stubbled skin.

"Where am I?" He glanced around the sunlit room where several other soldiers recuperated in hospital beds like his own.

"In the Franklin Hotel. The same US headquarters where Lola and Jacques found you. Jules and Pierrick brought you here. Do you remember how you saved him? He told us all about it. How he and four soldiers had been trapped in enemy crossfire. How you risked your life to save them. How you threw grenades to take out the Germans on one side, and the Russian Wolfhounds on the other. And how you did all that— despite being shot in your bad leg. Beau, I am so proud of you. And so very grateful that *you're alive*." Her sweet lips tasted like nectar as she gently pulled his into her own. "You kept your promise. You *survived*." She placed her hands on either side of head and kissed his brow. A warm tear streamed down her cheek and dropped onto his. "You came back to me. Oh, Beau...I am so glad you're alive!"

Zach licked his parched lips and asked for water, searching Yvette's pale, silvery gaze as she helped him drink from a cup.

When she set the glass down, he grabbed her hand

and cradled it between his own. He fervently kissed her slender fingers, his guttural voice cracking with grief. "I thought the Nazis had killed you." Throat constricting in anguish, Zach reached up to tenderly stroke the soft skin of her sublime, serene face. "Jules and I led a group of soldiers back to the Cancale garrison, but it was deserted. We infiltrated the farmhouse, but no one was there. When I saw a huge bloodstain on the floor, I thought it was yours. God, Yvette, I thought you were dead!" His breath ragged, he wrapped his arms around her neck and pulled her down onto his heaving chest, showering her dark, glorious curls with ardent kisses of overwhelming relief. "How did you escape?"

Yvette's forehead crumpled, and her lips quivered. "I killed the SS Officer in command. The monster who murdered my father and brothers. *Obersturmführer* Balsch. I shot him in the back of the head. It was his blood you saw on the floor." Fierce, feral fury blazed in her haunted gaze. "I finally avenged my family with his death."

Zach wiped a tear from her angry, flustered frown. "I'm glad you did. And incredibly grateful that you escaped. When I thought you were dead...I had nothing left to live for. But now, I do." He raised her hand to his lips and searched her silvery gaze. "You promised to marry me, Yvette Fleury. And I intend to make you keep your word."

Unbridled joy bloomed on her beautiful face.

When she leaned down to kiss him, he gently gripped the back of her head, tilting his own for better access to her voluptuous mouth. He slid his tongue between her plump lips, probing, penetrating, and reclaiming every tempting, tantalizing recess. And, although his bandaged leg inhibited movement, his healing body responded with eagerness and ardor. "I can't wait until we're alone. I want to ravish every inch of you." Zach groaned in her ear, relishing her requited moans of delight.

"Soon, my love. Very soon." Yvette pushed a strand of hair away from his brow, a mischievous glint emerging in her sparkling, silvery eyes. "I have something to tell you." A delicate fingertip traced his stubbled jaw. "You left me with a marvelous gift." She took his hand and placed it on her lower stomach, her eyes alight with wonder, her face aglow with delight.

Zach broke into a glorious grin as comprehension dawned. "You're pregnant?"

She nodded enthusiastically. "The baby will be born in the spring."

He pulled her into a bear hug, roaring with joy. "All the more reason to get married right away. Maybe a military chaplain can perform the ceremony."

"The Germans damaged the Saint-Vincent cathedral, but there's another lovely church, *l' Église Saint-Sauveur,* here in Saint-Malo that is still intact. It's near the beach, in the American controlled sector. I'd love to get married there, because of the symbolic name—the Church of the Sacred Savior. God saved you. For me. And our baby."

Zach smiled and kissed Yvette's hand. "Then that's where our wedding will be. As soon as Dr. Ferguson says I can leave." Fatigue settled over him like a thick, warm blanket. Despite his efforts to remain awake, his heavy eyelids drooped.

"*Dors, mon amour.* Sleep, my love. I'll be right here at your side." Yvette kissed his forehead, and a blissfully contented Zach drifted off to a deep, restorative sleep.

****

For two weeks, while Zach recuperated from surgery, performing therapeutic exercises to restore the strength in his leg, the medieval town of Saint-Malo was heavily bombed by Germans and Allies alike. Thick smoke filled the air as the city was consumed in flames. Finally, on the 17th of August 1944, the German commander, Colonel Von Aulock, surrendered the city of Saint-Malo to the American Forces.

Colonel Brett Lipscomb presented Zach with a purple heart for being wounded by the enemy during his valorous rescue of US infantrymen outside of Cancale.

Dr. Ferguson released him from the hospital, and Zach was granted an honorable discharge from the US Army. Although the surgery had been successful in saving Zach's leg, the sustained injuries would be permanent, leaving him unfit for duty. He would be able to walk and function normally, but with a limp for the remainder of his life.

On the second of September, the military garrison on the channel island of *Cézembre* surrendered, and the Battle of Saint-Malo was finally over.

And on the ninth of September, under a clear blue sky cleansed by the briny Breton breeze, Lieutenant Richard Zachford married Yvette Fleury in the quaint church of *l'Église Saint-Sauveur.*

After the modest ceremony, the newlyweds celebrated with family, friends, and military personnel in a local *brasserie*. As they sampled fresh seafood and gorged on the three-tiered wedding cake, Jules—the best man—proposed a toast. "To Yvette and Zach. Wishing you a lifetime of love and happiness together."

Amid joyous murmurs of *"Tchin-tchin,"* the wedding guests clinked their glasses of champagne, and Jules returned to his seat at the table of honor with Yvette and Zach.

Briac, Gwilherm, and Pierrick stuffed themselves with fresh oysters, scallops, and shrimp, while a smiling Lola rested her happy head on Jules' broad shoulder. Jacques, obviously enjoying the convivial camaraderie, chatted with members of the Free French Forces as they imbibed on celebratory champagne.

Her heart overflowing with happiness to be married to the man she loved, carrying his child, and celebrating the victory of the Battle of Saint-Malo, Yvette took a bite of cake as she listened to her brother Jules.

"There's so much damage to the city that the Allies are giving Saint-Malo back to France. We won the battle, but the seaport is useless for naval defense. The villagers are returning to their damaged homes—reuniting to remove the rubble and rebuild. Lola and I going to stay here and help with the restoration. When the war is over, we'll return to *le Vivier-Sur-Mer*." Jules hugged Lola to his side. "But, in the meantime, we'll be celebrating another wedding very soon."

Yvette smiled at her beloved brother, profoundly grateful that he had survived the gruesome battle. And brought a seriously wounded Beau back to her and their unborn child. "Beau and I plan to live in my cottage in the Breton woods. If you like, perhaps you and Lola could live in the farmhouse on the cliff. Restore our family home." Reaching across the table to squeeze Lola's hand, Yvette beamed at the dear old man she loved like a grandfather. "Jacques could return to the cabin and tend his sheep. We could all live close to one another. A big, happy extended family."

"I like that idea very much. Together, we'll recover from the horrors of war. Rebuild our city. Restore our homes. And celebrate the life we share." Jules raised his glass of champagne, prompting everyone at the table to do the same. "To the future. May it always be bright and full of hope."

As their friends cheered and clinked glasses, Yvette whispered to her new husband with eyes as blue as the Breton sea. "To our future, Beau. Together forever. Filled with love."

He flashed her a dazzling, disarming grin. "And to you, my beautiful, beguiling, beloved wife. *The Witch of the Breton Woods*."

A word about the author...

Jennifer Ivy Walker has an MA in French literature and is a professor of French at a state college in Florida.

Her novels encompass a love for French language, literature, and culture, incorporating her lifelong study and many trips to France.

Please visit the author here:

Website: https://jenniferivywalker.com/

Facebook: https://www.facebook.com/JenniferIvyWalker

Twitter: https://twitter.com/bohemienneivy

Instagram: https://www.instagram.com/jenniferivywalkerauthor/

Goodreads: https://www.goodreads.com/author/show/22671046.Jennifer_Ivy_Walker

Bookbub: https://www.bookbub.com/books/the-wild-rose-and-the-sea-raven-by-jennifer-ivy-walker

https://jenniferivywalker.com/